The Last Resort

The Last Resort

Stories

Jan Carson

doubleday
IRELAND

TRANSWORLD IRELAND

Penguin Random House Ireland, Morrison Chambers,
32 Nassau Street, Dublin 2, Ireland

www.transworldireland.ie

Transworld Ireland is part of the Penguin Random House group of companies
whose addresses can be found at global.penguinrandomhouse.com

Penguin
Random House
UK

First published in the UK and Ireland in 2020
by Transworld Ireland/Doubleday Ireland
an imprint of Transworld Publishers

A CIP catalogue record for this book
is available from the British Library.

ISBN 9781781620618

Typeset in 11.5/15.5 pt ITC Galliard Std
by Integra Software Services Pvt. Ltd, Pondicherry

Printed and bound in Great Britain by Clays Ltd, Elcograf S.p.A.

The authorized representative in the EEA is Penguin Random House Ireland,
Morrison Chambers, 32 Nassau Street, Dublin D02 YH68.

Penguin Random House is committed to a sustainable
future for our business, our readers and our planet. This book
is made from Forest Stewardship Council® certified paper.

MIX
Paper from
responsible sources
FSC® C018179

Written in Lockdown, conceived up the north coast with Hilary Copeland and Emma Must.

Contents

1

Pete

Frankie's rallied the troops. They're eager to get the show on the road. Frankie says he thinks the rain's for lifting. They all nod optimistically, though every one of them's dressed for a downpour. 'Happy' Trevor's in his wellies. The ladies are sporting Dunnes anoraks, hooded and zipped to the chin. They'd put you in mind of Teletubbies. But you wouldn't want to tell them that. Frankie has donned a fisherman's hat, the sort Oasis wore in the nineties. It sits high on his head like a loft extension. Given his age and the sombre occasion, it strikes me as somewhat undignified.

'Do you need a hand?' asks 'Happy' Trevor. I want to say, *of course I want a bloody hand*. It near killed me getting the bench out of the van. I had to roll it arse over end across the car park. It's still sitting where it landed, outside my caravan. I'd started picturing me out there in the summer, strumming the guitar while the sun went down. I mean, I probably wouldn't have bothered – I'd feel a right numpty singing, with this lot gawping through their curtains – but the idea of it appealed. Obviously, I knew the bench was Frankie's. It's his name on the wee brass plaque. *To Lynette. Always remembered. Love forever, Mum and Dad.* I knew he'd want it put somewhere meaningful. I just wasn't expecting him so soon.

We're only going two hundred yards, but Kathleen has packed for a day trip: tea in a flask and china mugs, sandwiches, traybakes, a first-aid kit. She's made her hubby bring his camera. 'Happy' Trevor looks suitably thrilled. She has him documenting everything for Frankie's sake. What's a blind fella going to do with photos? He's hardly going to frame them. If you ask me, the whole thing's a bit unhinged. But there's no point reasoning with this lot. You'd sooner turn the DUP.

Today's the first day of the season. It gets earlier every year. Most of the regulars will arrive later. The ones with kids, like Lois's lot, can't get down till after school. The retired contingent appeared before six: a.m. not p.m. (I kid you not.) They wanted to beat the traffic. The way they talk, you'd think it was nose to bumper from Dunsilly. It hasn't been like that for years. We'll be half empty till Easter. Ballycastle's a ghost town in winter. Anybody with sense or money'll take every opportunity to easyJet the hell out of Ulster. For forty quid you can half-term in a proper city, somewhere with fountains and decent wine. It's only the desperate and depraved who'd choose to spend February in a caravan. Muggins here doesn't have a choice.

I heard the oldies arriving in my dreams. Ford Mondeos reversing slowly. Kettles and hoovers grumbling. *Good Morning Ulster* on the radio. I should've been up. I'm meant to be responsible now. If I don't make an utter bollocks of this season, the whole shebang is coming to me. I'm not off to the best of starts. I was still flat out when Frankie appeared at my door. 'Are you up yet, son?' he shouted. 'It's today, so it is. When do you want to do the bench?'

He was all for starting then and there, at ten to seven in the dark. I fobbed him off with a mug of tea. While I was making it, I'd a stroke of genius. Pure hanging, I was – God knows where the idea came from – but I heard myself telling him Lynette would've wanted everybody there. We should wait till folks got their breakfasts in them. This seemed to sit well with Frankie. He took his tea and a chocolate digestive and plonked himself down on the bench to wait.

I felt awful, lying to him. I'd no notion what Lynette would want. She was well dead by the time I heard about her. My cousin Kevin filled me in the summer I turned nine. Dad buggered off that Christmas, leaving me and Mammy on our own. Uncle Jim had us down to Seacliff for the Twelfth fortnight. Uncle Jim's always been kind like that. Me and Kevin were in the car park kicking a football when he pointed out the scorch mark. 'That's where the wee girl exploded,' he told me. 'You weren't born back then.' After I found out about Lynette, I wouldn't do goalie any more. We always piled our jumpers up that end and I felt sick, standing where she'd died.

The rain definitely isn't lifting. I can feel it sogging through my jacket. 'Happy' Trevor's still waiting for an answer. *Do I want a hand with the bench?*

I'm not that fit at the best of times. After two months 'caretaking' – with nothing to do but eat and booze – I've gone to flab. I could seriously do with a hand. I consider my options. They're limited, to say the least. Frankie's blind. Trevor's pushing eighty. John has his hands full with the wife. She's clearly doting. Him and that woman Anna – the lonely-looking one in the cardigans – have her firmly clamped between them. You'd think Martha was about to bolt. There's a bad-tempered Yorkie to contend with and a quarter-mile of boggy field. God almighty, it's *Last of the Summer Wine* I've landed in.

'Naw, you're grand,' I say. 'I can manage.' I'd like to say 'Happy' Trevor looks relieved, but he's only got two facial expressions, both of which are scowls.

I haul one end of the bench on to my shoulder. My back makes a noise it's never made before. Now's the time to admit defeat. I could call Uncle Jim and ask him to send a cousin down. But the oldies are already falling in, forming a kind of cortège. Martha starts humming the funeral march. It's not her fault – she doesn't know where she is – but it isn't helping one wee bit. Frankie starts sniffling. 'Right, son,' he mumbles, 'let's take my wee girl home to rest.' Seemingly, this is a funeral now. I don't have the strength to object. 'Let's go,' I wheeze, and we're off. The back legs trail behind me, scooping two deep rivets out of the grass. Tomorrow, I'll have to come back and fix the mess. It's a nightmare being the responsible one.

Uncle Jim's left strict instructions: do whatever Frankie wants. He still feels bad about Lynette. She would've been turning fifty this year. Not that Jim could've stopped it. If anything, it's Frankie's fault. If you were in the RUC back then, you knew to be careful about your car. You didn't send your weans on ahead with the keys, even if you were on holidays. Frankie must know this himself. We're all here to help him but you can tell all the same the fella doesn't want helping. It's the pain that's keeping him alive.

Frankie wants Lynette's bench up on the cliff, so up on the cliff it'll have to go. Even if I wreck my back in the process. Even if it seems a bit demented, encouraging folks to sit up there, when the cliff's eroding. One false move and you'd be over the edge. Frankie claims Lynette liked the view: the sea and the scenery and all that. *Aye right*, she was fifteen when she died. What sort of teenager likes 'a view'? If I was older, or had more gumption, I'd level with him. I'd tell him to leave the bench down here, near the kiddies' playground, where everybody can get the good of it. I'd tell him it'd be symbolic: peace and children being the future and all that crap they put on murals now.

Maybe this is a kind of test, Uncle Jim's way of discovering whether I've got what it takes to run Seacliff. It's not too late for him to call things off, though it was only yesterday he dropped down the deeds. 'Think about it, son,' he said. 'I'd like to retire before the summer.' I haven't looked at them yet. It won't feel real till

I see my name there, next to 'owner'. I've been carrying the envelope around inside my jacket. I haven't opened it yet. I'm not ready for Seacliff to be real.

Do I have what it takes to step into Jim's shoes? Do I even want to try? Uncle Jim's the Richard Branson of our family. He has the barber's, a pub, two takeaways (Chinese and ordinary) and this site. He called it Seacliff because the sea can be seen from the cliff behind it. Uncle Jim hasn't a creative bone in his body. Nobody in our family does. Mammy's always wondering where I got the music from and why I couldn't have got something useful instead, something a bit more lucrative.

You'll be surprised to hear I had no great ambition to run a failing caravan park. Six months ago, I was all for leaving. London. Berlin. Amsterdam. I won't be telling Uncle Jim – he's big up in the Orange himself – but I got the Irish passport and everything. Sure, we'd no notion what Brexit was going to mean. There were mad rumours flying around. You'd need a visa to get down to Dublin. Derry was declaring independence. They were digging a moat around the border. I knew if I didn't leave soonish, I'd end up staying. Here, you either go when you're young, or you're stuck for good. I wanted to have a stab at the music. I wasn't Dylan or anything, but I'd a few good songs and a decent voice. If worst came to worst, I could do covers in the Irish bars. U2. Van. The Cranberries. Foreigners go mad for an Irish accent. Especially the Americans. They can't tell the difference between East Belfast and the wilds of Cork.

Then Uncle Jim had the stroke and the doctor told him to start thinking about early retirement. The pub and the barber's went to Kevin. My cousin Nigel got the takeaways. I wasn't expecting Jim to offer me Seacliff. If he'd gone about it any other way, I'd have been all, *thanks but no thanks, Uncle Jim.* But he made such a scene of it, standing up at the Christmas table, announcing that I was like a son to him and he wanted me to have a bit of his empire. Jesus, it was touching stuff. I was sat there, gurning in my cracker hat, and Mammy, she was gurning too. She hadn't looked that proud since I got my bronze Duke of Ed. After that, I could hardly tell them I was heading off.

There'll be no leaving now. Seacliff's got me. There's something stuck about this place. All the caravans here are statics; nobody's going anywhere fast. It already feels like the future is dragging me down. In fairness, it's probably just the bench. We've barely made it fifty yards and I'm dripping sweat. That big muscly boyo who's taken Marty McClintock's van comes out to see what the commotion's about. For a minute I think he's going to help, then he yells, 'Do the Parades Commission know about youse lot?' and cackles at his own wit.

'Bloody eejit,' mutters 'Happy' Trevor. I almost drop the bench. I can't believe the language on him. Him and Kathleen are good-living. She actually says 'crop' instead of 'crap'.

It's all too much for Frankie. He's started wailing like a child. Martha's doing her best to harmonize. I could weep myself, I'm that exhausted. I feel like that Greek lad shoving his boulder up the hill. How much longer is this going to take? I drop my end. I sit down to stretch the stiffness out of my back. Kathleen thinks we've paused for refreshments. She tells 'Happy' Trevor to start pouring the tea. Out come the buns and the egg salad sandwiches and, to be honest, I'm glad of the distraction. We huddle beneath golf umbrellas while Trevor prays for the food and the task ahead. I'm not what you'd call a religious man but at this stage, if the Good Lord wants to help, I'll not be laughing in his face.

Just as Trevor's labouring over his last Amen, a young fella comes out of the big green static. He does a double take when he spies us. He's not expecting a rake of oldies picnicking in the rain. He recovers quickly and asks what we're up to, then accepts a sandwich and a mug of tea. He offers Frankie his condolences and says – all casual like – 'Do you want a hand with that?' This is my Damascus moment. May the Good Lord forgive my unbelief. He's answered 'Happy' Trevor's prayer with a genuine angel. I'm so relieved, I almost cry. 'What about your good shoes?' asks Kathleen, for your man's all decked out in a swanky suit. He glances down as if he's forgotten what he's wearing. He shrugs. 'Sure, it's only a bit of mud.'

Richard – this is our angel's name – rolls up his sleeves. He positions himself at the bench's foot. We *one, two, three* and lift together. It's not half as heavy spread between two. We shuffle forwards through the field. The rain lifts a bit and it's kind of scenic. *I can do this*, I think. Not just the bench: the job, the site, the staying put. It was daft to think of leaving. I should be grateful to have this job.

When we get the bench positioned, I'm going to make an announcement. I'll wait till Frankie's said his piece and 'Happy' Trevor's done his sermon, then I'll tell them I'm taking over Seacliff. Saying it will make it real. Maybe I'll even sign the deeds up there, in a sort of symbolic way. The oldies'll like that, being included. They've been here since Seacliff began. I reach to check I have the deeds with me but my jacket pocket's empty. The envelope must have fallen out. It's that windy this morning, it'll be halfway to Scotland by now. I try to work myself up to feeling annoyed. But I'm not. I'm almost overcome with relief.

2

Lois

Nobody wants to sleep on the table. It used to be a
novelty, the kids' favourite feature of the caravan.
Anders had a whole palaver he'd go over: the table was
a Transformer. They needed to say the magic word
before it'd change into a bed. The kids are too cool
for table beds now. They want their privacy: a girls'
room and a separate room for Fergus. Besides, their
dad has taken the magic word back to Norway. I
can't figure out how to make the bed myself.

I sleep in the lounge, stretched out along the built-
in sofa. I'd be more comfortable on the floor. I hardly
sleep at all and, when I do, I always dream the bad
dreams. Down here, close to the ocean, they're more
real. It's the quiet. There are no car alarms or sirens, no
raised voices returning from the pub; nothing like
reality. There is the wind, the rain and the angry sea,
pitching itself against the cliff face. I know it can't be,

but this place always feels haunted, as if something or someone is watching me. Every night this week I've dreamt about slimy black creatures, faceless things with fins and scales. They crawl out of the sea to steal my children. I wake sweating in my sleeping bag and have to force myself not to check on them.

You don't have to be a psychologist to work out where the dreams come from. Take one comparative mythologist with a PhD in sea monsters. Add a traumatic divorce. Place in a godforsaken caravan site. Wait to see what unimaginable horrors emerge.

What did I think I was doing, dragging the kids down here for half-term? Who knows? It's me I feel sorry for, not them. They've another holiday coming. Their dad's whisking them off to Bali for Easter. I can't afford anything except Granny's caravan. Orla's never done reminding me how crap it is. Bali will be paradise after Ballycastle. Anders wins again. The salary he's on, he can afford to spoil them. Norwegian universities hand out tenure like it's going out of fashion. In Belfast you're lucky to get a couple of undergrad tutorials and a pass for the staff canteen. I'd go down the research route but they're not exactly tripping over themselves to fund research into things that go bump at the bottom of the sea. Anders, on the other hand, had no problem securing funding for his research into the Jörmungandr. He's some pup, that Jörmungandr; the Norse equivalent of the Kraken. The second he lets go of his tail, the world's going to end. Anders left me two days after he got the Jörmungandr gig. There's a metaphor in there somewhere.

While we're on the subject of metaphors, let me present the static caravan. If you're being technical, it's an oxymoron. A caravan's meant to make you mobile. But this one's static, which means, despite my best intentions, I am perpetually stuck. It didn't always feel like this. We used to have good times here. Anders and I would take turns minding the kids so we could work on our PhDs. We brought them down to hunt monsters in the caves. I didn't realize it, but those were our best times. Back then, the future felt infinite. The kids aren't little any more. They're not interested in ploutering round windswept beaches, searching for kelpies and selkies or whatever mad thing their mammy's researching this week. They want high-speed broadband, Starbucks and their mates. I can hardly blame them. Alma's eleven now. Fergus and Orla are nearly fourteen. Gone are the days when they'd run screaming in delight at the mere mention of a Grindylow emerging from the water to grab an unsuspecting child's ankle. The Grindylows in *Harry Potter* gave them a bit of extra mileage, but the twins are well over Harry now. Alma won't be far behind.

My kids have grown up. They're no longer afraid of unbelievable things. Now their fears are sharp and specific. Who will Alma run around with in big school? What if nobody watches Orla's YouTube channel? Do I think Dad'll get a new family in Oslo? Now, it's only me who dreams about monsters. I don't know what to do with my fears. I don't know how to get over them.

I can't get back to sleep this morning. I get up and make coffee, moving quietly around the tiny kitchen so as not to wake the kids. I find my wellies and go out for a smoke. I vape in front of the kids and say I've given up proper smoking. I was actually quitting, until Anders left. Ever since, I've kept an emergency packet in my coat pocket. I'm careful not to reach for it when they're watching. Fergus and Orla are easily fooled. Alma's different. Alma's like me. She sees everything, even the things she doesn't see.

It's not even six, but next door John and Martha are already up. I can see the two of them moving around behind the curtains, like shadow puppets dancing in the pale blond light. Old people rise early, but even for old folk half five's a shocking sort of time to be up. I wonder if everything's all right.

I take my cigarettes down to the cliff edge. There's a bench here now, a memorial to that girl who died in the car bomb. That was a bit before my time. It's not the safest in the dark but it's nice to have a place to sit. Everybody's talking about the cliff eroding. A whole section's crumbled away since last year. The new caretaker's been round to tell the children they're not to go near the cliff. It isn't stable. I've also read them the Riot Act, but I can't seem to keep away myself. It's the sea. It drags me in.

It's forty years since I fell in love with my first sea monster: Jonah's whale in the illustrated Bible. I made Dad read the same story every night for months. I'd no interest in Daniel in the lions' den or any of Jesus's snazzy miracles. It was the whale that fascinated me: the idea that there were all sorts of strange creatures swimming around beneath the surface. It scared me, imagining monstrous things, down there in the soupy dark. I liked that kind of fear. It reminded me that I was small. There were so many things left to discover. I'm not small any more but the world still feels massive. It's so much harder to be brave on your own.

I've been collecting sea monsters my whole life. Selkies. Sirens. Naiads. Nessie. Tiamat. And the Kraken himself. I've made a career out of it, if you could call three published articles an academic career. (Anders clearly didn't.) There's a sea monster in almost every oral tradition. I'm never done discovering new ones. I can't explain what draws me to them, but I am drawn, lured in like one of those shipwrecked sailors who tried to resist the Sirens' call. I'm only content when I'm near the ocean, looking for God only knows what. It's not like I actually believe there's anything out there. It isn't my job to believe. I'm only here to record the stories. I'm always on the periphery.

Even though it's still dark I can see for miles, all the way out to the lighthouses blinking on Rathlin Island. There's hardly any light pollution. The stars seem brighter than the city stars. The sky's a softer shade of black. I take my mobile out and turn on the torch. I drag the beam slowly across the sea's surface. The light catches and lingers on the waves' white crests. It's choppy out there. It always is in February. I'm searching for the Scottish sea monster. It's a force of habit. Every time we come to Seacliff – and we've been coming since before the twins were born – we have to look for the Scottish sea monster. It's a family tradition. I can't help myself.

Everybody has their own favourite myth. Ours is the story of the German U-boat captain who abandoned ship off Scotland in 1918. Looking to save face, he claimed to have been attacked by a sea monster with large eyes set in a horny sort of skull, and teeth that could be seen glistening in the moonlight. When pushed by the British officers who captured him, Captain Krech provided an artist's impression of the beast. It looked a lot like Nessie. Which, given the location, made total sense. It's a tall tale, now discredited, but the first time Anders recounted it, screwing up his big blond face to make a monster of himself, my children took to it as if it was their very own origin myth. School projects ensued, monster portraits rendered in crayon, plasticine and poster paint. Then, finally, a fact-finding trip to Stranraer when the U-boat surfaced five years ago. No visit to Granny's caravan was ever complete without a midnight expedition to hunt our sea monster. For a while, Anders and I thought we'd spawned three more comparative mythologists. Then the hormones kicked in.

I tried to bring them up here last night. I wanted to do something together for a change. The three of them were plugged into their devices: headphoned and staring at their various screens. I thought I'd feel closer to them, down here in the caravan. Instead, it's felt more like they're drifting away. They only take their headphones out to eat or complain about the crappy Wi-Fi. Fergus won't look me in the eye. Orla talks like a text message. *Hashtag this. LOL that. OMG Mum feel wick for you.* This being exactly what she said last night, when I suggested putting on our coats and going for a midnight monster hunt. Even my baby's not a baby any more. I went up to the cliff edge alone. I brought hot chocolate in a Thermos mug and tried to pretend it was an adventure. It wasn't a game without them. I felt like they'd all moved on and left me behind. I stared down into the ocean. It didn't look familiar, only angry and a little threatening. When I came stomping back down from the cliff, it was easy to spot our caravan. There was a pale blue light coming off the kids' iPads. The whole caravan glowed eerily as if someone inside was on a sunbed.

Our caravan's still dark this morning. It'll be after ten before the teenagers emerge and start plugging in. The forecast's for rain. The forecast's always for bloody rain. We'll be cooped up all day, sniping at each other. I'm looking at the dark silhouette of our caravan, wondering if we should just pack up and head home, when a light begins bobbling towards me. At first I think it's one of the kids, come to share a bad dream or demand breakfast pancakes like they used to when they were wee.

As the light gets closer, I see it's only Pete, the care-taker, using his mobile as a torch. 'Hey,' he says as he approaches, 'you're up early.' I tell him I couldn't sleep. I've come down here for a minute's peace. You know what it's like with teenagers. I look at Pete. In his hoodie and board shorts. He looks like an overgrown student. I'm guessing he has no idea what it's like with teenagers. He sits down next to me on the bench and says he's on the prowl. Things are going missing around

the site. He's lost some important documents. Somebody else is missing golf clubs. It's his first weekend in
charge of Seacliff. A crime wave won't reflect well on
him. He asks if I've seen anything suspicious. 'Only the
sea monster,' I say. It sounds like a joke inside my head
but Pete stares at me like I'm mad. I try to apologize,
to explain without sounding even more unhinged that
there's a Scottish sea monster in Beaufort's Dyke and
hunting it is a family tradition. My kids are dead into
monsters. They think they are tremendous craic.

I'm not convincing Pete. I'm not even convincing
myself. In our awkwardness we turn and peer out to
sea. I let the beam from my phone sweep languidly
across the waves and for a second, just a heartbeat
moment, an immense creature breaks the surface and
arches itself upwards. I see large eyes set in a horny
sort of skull and teeth that glisten in the moonlight.
Then the creature ducks back beneath the waves and I
can't be certain I've seen anything. It could be a sign;
after all these years, an acknowledgement that I'm not
alone. More likely I'm just hallucinating. I'm seeing
what I want to see, when I should be giving the kids
my full attention. The kids I have, not the kids I want
them to be.

I glance over at Pete. He can't have seen it. He's
already walking away. When I return to the caravan,
Orla's up and raising hell. The iPads are missing, and
their mobiles. Orla is hysterical. She wants to call her
dad in Oslo. She wants him to come and take her away.
I should sit them down and let them vent. I should
admit that Seacliff's not working. We could be back in

Belfast before lunch. Instead, I make angry, spite-filled pancakes and fish the Scrabble board out of the cup-board. I paste a smug grin on to my face and I tell my beautiful, furious children that I'm glad all their screens have been stolen because it means we get to make our own fun now.

3

Richard

I should have brought a tape measure from home. I keep meaning to. Instead I'm measuring the caravan the old-fashioned way: pacing slowly round the outside, counting every step. It's thirty-six size nines from end to end. This makes no sense. I've just measured the inside. Sixty-eight steps. Almost twice as long. I've repeated the whole process three times, just to be sure. I'm no maths genius, but I can see something's not adding up. The caravan's twice as big inside as outside. It's basically a Tardis.

The concept of a Tardis isn't the easiest to understand if you're not familiar with *Doctor Who*. 'Bigger inside than outside,' I try to explain to the clients. 'You know, like Mary Poppins's handbag, or Oscar the Grouch's bin on *Sesame Street*, or maybe God.' (*Is there more to God than we know about? I kind of hope so.*) The clients look at me, baffled. Most of them don't have much English.

I still call them clients down here. It's important to keep things professional. *Professional, my arse.* I've broken every rule in the book: driving them to Seacliff, sneaking them past Pete, letting them stay in my parents' ancient static. If my boss found out, I'd never work in the sector again. I could claim they'd nowhere else to go and the caravan's just lying here, empty. I could make a whole song and dance about common sense and human decency, but we're not living in an age of common sense or decency. It's all red tape and risk assessments these days. I can't hide sixteen homeless men in a static caravan and not expect a roasting when I'm caught.

I say when, not if. I can't see myself getting away with this much longer. It's two days since I got caught up in helping the oldies install that memorial bench for the dead girl. Ever since, I've felt like somebody's got their eye on me. The caravan's doing its best to help. It's colluding in my schemes. Every time I drop a new fella off, it's expanded to make more room. At first, I thought it was an optical illusion. My clients are the sort of men who know how to make themselves look small. But now, I'm sure something weird's going on. The static's just as roomy as the night I dropped Samir off. I told him it was only a temporary fix, till he got over his flu. That was six weeks ago. There's sixteen of them now. Word's got out. They keep sidling up to me in the drop-in. *Richard, we hear you have a place.* I'm too soft. I can't help it. Especially now the weather's turned. It's been lashing since Christmas and the hostels are bunged. I can't say no. At least, not while the caravan keeps stretching like a one-size-fits-all jumper. There's something about Seacliff which seems to suit the clients. This is an end-of-the-road kind of place.

I've come down early this evening to measure the caravan again. I've paced my way through sleeping bags, backpacks and prayer mats. It's definitely sixty-eight steps. I'm just measuring outside one last time before I head home. It's getting late. Mum fusses about me working too much. Dad doesn't. I'm a chip off the old block. A workaholic, he means. He's proud of this. I spend half my life trying not to disappoint him.

I've already changed into my suit. I used the caravan's tiny bathroom. It stinks in there; hardly surprising, what with sixteen men cooped up together. Fragrant's what we call it in work and try to coerce the clients into the shower twice a week. Sometimes, when I get home, I can still smell them on me. I'm used to it. It's who I am now. But I can't have Dad asking questions. I always carry a business suit inside the flashy briefcase he bought me for graduation. My brothers all have the same one: Philip, the actuary, Matthew, the financial analyst, and Stephen, who's taking his bar exams. My initials are engraved on the lock. Dad thinks I use it to transport papers to council meetings. In his head I'll be clutching it when I make Chief Exec round about the time I turn thirty. My dad has high expectations for me.

By the time Dad turned thirty he already had six businesses on the go. The caravan was a present for my mum, something to make up for all the long nights in the office. It was the eighties. Northern Ireland wasn't like it is now. Nobody wanted to be in Belfast with the bombs going off and the soldiers stationed on every other corner. A caravan on the North Coast was the height of luxury, somewhere you could escape to at the weekend. They felt safe here. Or they did until that bomb went off in the car park. Dad says Mum cried for a week about the wee girl. I wasn't born then, but it could easily have been one of my brothers. The swings were right beside the policeman's car. After that Dad bought the villa in Portugal and they quit coming down to Seacliff. My brothers used the caravan for boozy weekends with their mates. They talked about slumming it with the common people. It was a novelty to them: eating fish suppers with their fingers, playing the slots in Barry's Amusements, picking up local girls in hotel discos. Staying in a caravan. For a while it was a laugh. Then they lost interest. The caravan got shabby. It's only me who comes here now. Me, and my sixteen mates who've got nowhere else to go.

I couldn't tell Dad about them. I've never even told him what I really do. He wouldn't understand. In his world, you work hard, and you do well. There's no reason to end up on the street, hawking *The Big Issue*, unless you've brought it on yourself. In Dad's book, lazy's the absolute worst thing you can be. He's not a monster or anything. He's actually very generous. He donates huge amounts to charity every year. He's always in the *Tatler*, grinning, next to one of those outsized cheques. He gives to cancer, old people and children in impoverished countries. These are the kinds of people who deserve his help. They're unfortunate rather than lazy. Dad has no time for what I do. Enabling, he calls it. He votes for the party who don't do handouts. He'd have a pink fit if he could see my clients lying about his caravan, contributing nothing worthwhile to society.

I suppose I've been taking the cowardly option. I don't go out of my way to lie to Dad. I just let him believe what he wants to believe. The longer it goes on, the harder it is to tell him. How would I even begin? *Hey, Dad, you know the way I'm climbing the local government career ladder? Well, I'm not. I'm actually a caseworker down at the homeless shelter. I make sixteen grand a year before tax. And I'm happy.* He'd have the meltdown to end all meltdowns, even worse than the Christmas our Matthew came out. Best not to say anything. Every day, before I leave work, I nip into the staff loos to swap my polo shirt and joggers for a suit. I come in the front door swinging my briefcase, looking every inch the junior exec. I'm not lying to my parents. I'm not telling the whole truth either.

I'm on my fourth lap of the caravan when I notice the girl next door. She's staring at me from behind the curtains. I must look like a right eejit pacing about in the dark. There's three kids in that caravan – teenagers, really – and one of those over-earnest mums who tries to engage them in outdoor pursuits. The dad's not on the scene any more. I've seen the kids around the site, holding their mobiles aloft, trying to pick up a clear signal. On Friday I had words with the boy. He was chasing the 4G close to the cliff edge. That cliff's not stable; why they put that bench up there I do not know.

I'm pretty sure the whole site'll be condemned soon. Knowing this makes me feel better about letting the clients use Dad's caravan. They might as well get the good of it while it's still here. All that to say the boy didn't appreciate me telling him off.

His sister's giving me the evil eye now. I wave at her. She draws back from the window and disappears. I assume she's mortified to be caught staring. I assume wrong. Thirty seconds later she's outside, sitting on the caravan's steps. She's wearing pyjamas beneath her anorak and clutching a notebook. She looks like one of Dad's secretaries: young, slightly furious, permanently poised to take dictation. 'What are you doing?' she asks, and I say, 'Nothing.' She notes this down. She claims to have been watching me for the last fifteen minutes. 'You look very suspicious,' she says, and, before I can protest, launches into a spiel. Apparently, there's been a spate of thefts: important documents, her iPad, her brother's and sister's mobiles, golf clubs, a couple of pictures. She suspects some sort of international crime syndicate. She's heard people muttering in different languages. Now, here I am, creeping about in the dark, dressed up like a James Bond villain. I have to admit, it doesn't look good.

'Hold your horses there, Nancy Drew,' I say. She frowns. The joke's lost on her. She's too young. 'It's my caravan. I can walk around it all night if I want to.'

'It's not,' the girl says. 'It belongs to that other fella. The foreign one I've seen going in and out.'

So, this is it? I've been scuppered by a child with a Hello Kitty notebook. She'll tell her mum about the men. Maybe she already has. The mother'll tell Pete. He'll phone the contact on my lease, which isn't me. Dad will have a canary. I'll be out on my ear before next weekend. Me and the clients will be in the same boat then. Nowhere to go. Not even a magic caravan to fall back on. I think quickly. Maybe I can appeal to her benevolent side. Wee girls love an underdog, something to take pity on. There's not a huge difference between a stray kitten and a rake of homeless men. I wouldn't even have to exaggerate. Most of my clients have been to hell and back. The least they deserve is a few weeks by the sea. I look at the girl. She glares back. I can tell from the way her jaw's set she's not going to buy a sob story. She looks like Dad when he's closing a deal. I change tack.

'Aye,' I say, lying through my teeth, 'that was my mate Jason you saw. He's looking after the place for me. That's allowed. It's my caravan.'

She writes this down, glances at her notes, then up at me. 'Is Jason robbing people's stuff?'

It's not the first time I've had to answer this question. People are always flinging accusations at my clients. Sometimes they stick. Sometimes they don't. Occasionally they're justified; only very occasionally. I try not to lose my temper. I look straight at the girl. 'You can't go round accusing people of stealing,' I say firmly. 'You haven't got any evidence.'

'I've been watching your caravan,' she says pointedly, 'really closely.' She leaves the statement hanging. It's like a tiny bomb, sitting there, just waiting to go off.

I try to remember I'm the adult here. I shouldn't let a child intimidate me. Then again, I let everybody boss me around. I square my shoulders inside my suit. Dad says a defined shoulder projects authority. I swallow the dry lump in my throat. 'And, what have you seen?' I ask.

The girl consults her notebook. I'm waiting for her to list the men I've brought down late at night, all their worldly possessions shoved into Tesco carriers. Any second now she'll ask who they are, where they've come from and how on earth they're all fitting inside that caravan. But she doesn't. She just fixes her big, serious eyes on me and says, 'I've not seen anything *yet*. But I'm still watching.'

The relief makes me cocky. 'Watch away. You'll not see anything suspicious,' I say. 'It's just an ordinary caravan.' I'm tempted to invite her inside to see for herself. I'm certain the caravan won't let me down. It'll pull whatever magic manoeuvre's required to convince the girl that this is an ordinary static with perfectly plausible dimensions and nothing at all to hide. No shapeshifting walls. No expanding ceiling. No homeless men hiding. We're on the same team, me and the caravan. It understands what I'm doing with the clients. This is who I am.

The girl's lost interest, or maybe the cold is getting to her. She goes back inside and closes the door. The caravan still looks cavernous. I could measure again but I'm running late. I tell the clients to be more careful. Stay inside and watch out for the nosy kid next door. I'll be back with food tomorrow evening. I go to grab my briefcase from the table. It isn't there. I look all around the caravan. It's disappeared. Dad's going to ask me where it's gone. This could be my chance to level with him. I could say, *Dad, there's something I need to tell you. I'm never going to be like you.* Or I could just tell him I've left it in the office. *Office it is.* I haven't the energy for a scene. All sixteen of the clients are adamant they haven't touched my briefcase. I want to believe them. I honestly do.

4

Anna

Pointless has just started when somebody hits the caravan door a wild clatter. 'Who's that?' snaps Mummy. I want to say, *how should I know?* What I actually say is, 'I'll just go and see.' I'm forty-seven but I still wouldn't dare give her lip. Mummy gives me a right pissy look. She hates being disturbed during *Pointless*. She used to time the dinner round it. We'd sit on the sofa eating off trays while she shouted her answers at the screen. If I sat too close, I'd get showered in mashed potato; too far away, and I couldn't reach to feed her. Mummy doesn't eat dinner any more. She's had no appetite since she died. Doesn't stop her watching *Pointless*, though, or insisting I have my dinner while it's on.

It's only five o'clock. Nobody wants their dinner at five. On the Continent they're just rising from lunch. Not that I've ever been to the Continent. Mummy

didn't approve of it. We always took our holidays in
Ayr. She liked Ayr. It was just as bleak as Ballycastle but
they'd a sea you could look at through the rain. Now
she's gone, there's nothing keeping me from the Continent. Only she's not really gone, is she? She's still
here, following me round the bungalow, nagging.
Dragging me to church. Demanding we head down to
the caravan every weekend. Nothing's changed. Nothing's ever going to change. Nobody else can see
Mummy. But I can. And she's doing my head in.

   I set my tray aside. I cross the caravan to the door.
Maggie waddles behind me, winding her fat body
round my slippers. She's not as fast as she once was,
though she stills manages to trip me up two or three
times a day. That wee dog has a murderous streak in
her. She's made it abundantly clear I'm no substitute
for Mummy. She's called after Maggie Thatcher.
Mummy was a big fan of the Iron Lady; she'd the hair
done like her and all. The dog takes after her namesake.
She won't do anything she doesn't want to, dying being
the first thing that comes to mind. Maggie's nineteen
now: human years, not dog ones. That's ancient for a
Yorkie. I'm starting to wonder if she might be immortal
too. If it wasn't for Maggie, I wouldn't be tied to Seacliff. I could go anywhere I wanted: Spain, Portugal,
even the States. I've a cousin out there, in Kentucky.
I could finally be shot of Mummy. But I can't leave. I
promised her I'd take care of Maggie. I thought she'd
go soon after Mummy. Here we are, three years later,
two bitter old bitches in a caravan, pandering to a dead
woman's every whim.

There are three children at the door: two girls and a sullen-looking lad. They belong to the woman in the through-other caravan next to John and Martha's. She does something at Queen's: research into weird myths. Mummy says it's satanic. She used to make me shove Bible tracts under their door. The children certainly aren't Protestant-looking. The wee one hasn't seen a comb in weeks. I hold the door at an angle and peek at them through the slit. I don't want them seeing into the lounge. I'm pretty sure Mummy's only visible to me, but you never know with children. They're more susceptible to the things beyond.

The wee one speaks first. 'Can your dog come out to play with us?'

I glance down at Maggie. Never has a dog looked less interested in playing. 'Maggie's very old,' I say. 'She doesn't really play any more.'

'Can we take her for a walk, then, just up to the bench and back?'

I've no weans myself – that boat sailed years ago – but I know it's not safe to let children go wandering about in the dark, especially with the cliff in the state it's in. I try to sound friendly, explaining this. Even though they're only here for Maggie, it's nice to talk to somebody who isn't dead or halfway there. When I'm not stuck in the caravan with Mummy, I'm next door keeping an eye on Martha. You don't get much sense out of her these days.

If it wasn't for Mummy, and the creeping suspicion I might look like a paedophile, I'd ask the weans in. We could raid the biscuit tin, maybe play I Spy, for there's no playing cards in our caravan. Mummy calls them the Devil's cards. She lost an uncle once to gambling and afterwards banned all associated activities. Everything from Snap to Seacliff's summer bingo sessions was outlawed. We'd sit in our caravan with the windows open, listening to country gospel tapes while all the normal people played bingo in the rec room. I was jealous of the bingo people, even though I knew they were going to Hell for it. They sounded like they were having fun. Mummy doesn't approve of fun. Not even on holidays.

The children have no interest in spending time with me. They're bored, but not *that* bored. The wee one says she'll come back for Maggie tomorrow. It's a statement, not a question. I can't get over the cut of her, standing here talking down to an adult. She's still got cartoon ducks on her wellies. She can't be much more than ten. Mummy despises children like this. Bold children. Forward children. Children with notions. Not me. I wish I'd an ounce of her confidence. I'd turn on my heels and go back inside and tell Mummy I'd had enough. I'd move out. Sell the bungalow. Sell the caravan. Do something about the stupid dog.

Maggie's itching to get out. She's looking for a walk. I take her out to do her business after *Pointless* so she's in and settled before the news comes on. Mummy never misses the news. She says it's so she can pray more effectively for people suffering in the world. Mummy's not interested in the suffering people anywhere further south than Newry. She makes a point of switching from UTV to BBC so she gets two doses of the local news. Everybody round here's the same. They can't see past the end of their noses. I suppose I'm no better myself. I've been stuck in a rut since the day I was born. In the lounge behind me, I hear Mummy fumbling for the remote. Any second now, she's going to shout, 'Close that door, Anna! You're letting all the heat out.' I can't risk the children hearing. The wee one looks like the sort of child who asks a lot of questions.

I mumble something about having to look after the dog myself. I say I'm sorry. I try to close the door and, simultaneously, push Maggie back inside. The child wedges a single yellow boot in the door. She looks ferocious, not unlike Mummy in one of her moods. 'Things are going missing round here,' she says. 'If I were you, I'd keep a close eye on that dog of yours.' Then she pulls her foot out sharply and the door slams shut. I stand there for a second, mesmerized. I can still see the pink blur of their faces, pixelated behind the frosted glass. *Have I just been threatened by a ten-year-old?* I think I have. The disturbing thing is I feel no inclination to stand up for myself. Mummy has me worn down. Anybody can have a punt at me now; anybody at all.

Mummy asks who was at the door. I lie. I'm not sure why I lie. Maybe I'm scundered that I've let myself be bullied by a child. I tell her it was Pete, the caretaker, warning me about burglaries on site. I get a mouthful then, a five-minute rant about slipping standards. Seacliff isn't what it used to be back in the day, when it was full of nice Christian families and they'd open-air meetings on the bowling lawn. Mummy says there's a wicked presence about the place. She says she's seen foreign fellas sneaking about. She must be delusional. There's no foreign fellas in Seacliff. Sure, what would they be doing in Ballycastle, in February, in the rain? She turns her attention back to the telly. There's a round on Agatha Christie. Mummy's in her element. As soon as *Pointless* is over she tells me to take Maggie out. As always, I do exactly as I'm told.

I don't put her on the lead. Maggie's the only dog on site and she's too old to wander far. I walk behind the caravan and along the cliff, keeping away from the edge. Even in the dark I can see the ground is crumbling. It's getting closer and closer to the caravans. The empty one, at the end of the row, is only a few feet from the edge now. There's something weird about that caravan. There's nobody in it, but when I'm up there, I always feel like I'm being watched. I'm probably just paranoid. Though Mummy's right, there's a rougher element in Seacliff these days. You should see the big beefy fella in Marty McClintock's van. He's absolutely covered in tattoos.

Maggie toddles along behind me, sniffing and pausing to dribble on the grass. Sometimes she veers dangerously close to the edge. I've nothing against her. As far as dogs go, Maggie's grand, and there's been times when Mummy's tearing strips off her that I've even felt a bit of solidarity. But, if she were to totter over the cliff's edge, would that be such an awful thing? There are worse ways for a nineteen-year-old dog to go. On a selfish note, it'd free me up. At least, I tell myself it would.

Would it really? I doubt it. The problem is Mummy's got to me. She's spent so long telling me I can't manage myself I've actually started believing her. I'm a homebird. I'm not cut out for socializing. And, when it comes to men...Well, Mummy says there's no point setting myself up for a disappointment. I'd like to have got married, maybe even had weans. For a while I was seeing Leonard from church. He wasn't good-looking or anything, but he was awful kind. And he'd his own house and the plumbing business. I could've been happy with Leonard but he wanted to get married right away. I couldn't abandon Mummy. It wouldn't have been right. Those last few years she needed me for everything. Feeding. Bathing. Helping her to the toilet. Leonard said I needed to draw a line. Mummy was asking too much of me. Leonard's with Michelle now. She's younger. They've a wee one on the way. I'm happy for them. At least, I'm trying to be. It's too late for me to be happy myself. I'll be fifty soon. I'll hardly be making any big changes now.

There's a word for the day after tomorrow: overmorrow. It was on *Eggheads* yesterday. I'm forever accumulating useless facts off Mummy's programmes. I've been thinking about overmorrow all day. It's depressing me. Nothing's going to change tomorrow or the day after or any time soon. What have I got to look forward to? Work. Church. Home. Caravan at the weekend. Same old, same old for the next thirty years. Then eternity with God and Mummy. Hopefully God'll stick us in different bits of Heaven. Knowing my luck, we'll be sharing a caravan.

I'm standing on the clifftop, right in front of poor Lynette's bench, feeling sorry for myself, when the

foreign fella grabs me from behind. I don't hear him.
I don't see him. One second I'm alone in the dark,
the next I'm being dragged backwards by the shoulders. Everything happens so quickly I don't even think
to scream.

'I got you,' says the man. He speaks English with an
accent: Polish maybe, or Romanian.

I turn to look at his pale face looming out of the
dark. He looks straight at me. I recognize that look.
It's the way people always look at me: Leonard,
Michelle, the girls in work. This stranger pities me. He
sees a frumpy, middle-aged woman standing alone on
a cliff edge looking sad, and he's made the assumption
most people would make. I'm mortified. I begin to
mumble incoherently. 'I wasn't…I wouldn't…I'm
just out here walking my dog.'

The man's embarrassed too. He's misread the situation. Or perhaps he hasn't. He doesn't know how you
move away from a cliff edge. He seizes upon the dog.

'You're walking dog?' he repeats desperately. We're
both clinging to this line.

'Yes,' I say. 'Maggie. My mother's dog.'

'Where is dog?'

I look around. Maggie's nowhere to be found. I call
her name. She usually comes when I call. Tonight, she
doesn't. I know, instantly, we won't find her. Maggie's
gone. She's toddled over the cliff or those horrible children have taken her. Still, I let the man help me search.
Anything to delay the moment when I have to tell
Mummy I've lost her dog. She'll go ballistic. Even *The
One Show* won't be able to distract her and Mummy

never misses *The One Show*, although she says it's not the same since Christine whatsername went over to *Loose Women*. (Mummy doesn't approve of *Loose Women*, neither the concept nor the show.)

We spend ages searching for Maggie. We go all the way around the site. The man's English isn't great and I've no idea what he's doing here. But he is kind and I am grateful for this. I won't tell Mummy about him. It'd be nice to have something of my own. Beneath my anorak, my shoulders are still throbbing where he grabbed me. It is years since anyone touched me. Literally years. I wonder if he's left a mark.

5

Vidas

The second I empty my backpack I notice Tetis's tool belt is missing. It's not hard to keep track of my possessions. Everything fits in a single bag. My passport, with its burgundy cover. The picture of my parents' wedding. Clothes and toiletries. Two fat Stephen King novels Richard lent me. My English isn't bad, but there's room for improvement. Richard keeps telling me to read more. There's nothing else to do in this place. We must stay inside the caravan. He'll get in trouble if anyone spots us. I feel bad. I have not been careful. I get bored and go walking late at night. Richard's all about helping people. I could tell him I've been helping too: poor old Frankie and that sad-looking lady last night on the cliff. If I hadn't been there to stop her, who knows what she'd have done. The truth is I can't breathe inside this caravan. Every day the walls keep coming in. Will I ever get away from here?

The other men are better at passing the time. They play cards or write in the journals their caseworkers have given them. They tell us writing's good for our mental health. Writing. Drawing. Talking about our feelings. *What's the point?* A job's the only thing that would make me feel better. A good job and a decent place to live. I'm not complaining about the caravan. Richard's risked his job, sneaking us on to the site. It might be cramped and smelly, but it's no worse than the hostel and a million times better than sleeping outside in February. And there's the sea. Every morning I wake to the waves crashing against the cliff. God, I've missed the sea. When you grow up in a city like Klaipėda the ocean's in your blood. It soothes you.

I check under my sleeping bag. I turn my backpack inside out, just to be sure. Yusef is dozing next to me. I ask if he's seen the tool belt. 'It's important,' I say. 'My grandfather gave it to me.' He shrugs, pretending he doesn't understand, then goes back to sleep. I don't blame him. I've done the same myself. The shrug. The baffled look. *Sorry, no English.* Sometimes, it's easier this way. Yusef isn't the problem. He's *dead on*, as they say in Belfast. We worked together on the building site and got laid off on the same day. I'm not so sure about the others. I don't trust them yet. Tetis brought me up to see the good in everyone. He always gave his workers chances they didn't deserve. He used to take men on straight out of prison, no references required. People thought he was soft, but he wasn't. He saw potential in his workers, sometimes before they saw it themselves. I used to be more like Tetis. It was easier to trust people back home.

It's hard to trust these men. They're from nine different countries, none of them mine. How can they be anything but strangers when we can't talk? We've only got a few shared words. We do our best. Pointing. Signing. Scribbling pictures on paper like children playing a game. Down here, I feel a child. It's like being on holidays; a horrible, never-ending holiday. Sleeping on the floor. Washing out of a bucket. Playing cards. Endlessly playing cards. If I play one more game of poker, I'm going to scream. Something about this place is stuck. This is not a useful way to live. It is wrong to make a person feel this useless. I should write that in my journal. It is exactly the kind of shit caseworkers love.

My journal's long gone. I swapped it with a Syrian man for a thing of shower gel. *Minty fresh.* The shower gel ran out weeks ago. Now I'm using dish soap. My hair feels like it doesn't belong to my head. When you're homeless in somebody else's country, nothing feels like it belongs to you. You don't even belong to yourself any more. You're not allowed to settle. You can't point to the past and say, *look at my roots running deep in this place; don't even think about moving me on.* Even here, by the sea – the same sea that runs into the Baltic – I don't belong. It is not my place. I am nothing here. The things I've brought from home are all that's left of me.

I could cause a fuss about my tool belt; start yelling and flinging accusations round the caravan. I know one of them must've stolen it. My tool belt deserves a fuss. Tetis gave me it the day I left Klaipėda. He wanted me to have his tools. My grandfather didn't understand why I was leaving. Ambition meant nothing to him. As long as he had enough to look after his family, he was happy. I was different. I wanted a degree so I could call myself a civil engineer. It would take years saving up in Lithuania. In Britain I could work and save my tuition fees quickly. Nobody in our family had a degree. Not even Tetis. It didn't matter that he owned his own business and employed dozens of men. Without a degree, he was still just a builder in my eyes, a common tradesman. I wanted to be something better. God, I was arrogant back then. But Tetis never tried to stop me. 'Go,' he said, 'see the world. When you're ready, come back. I'll be here.'

I left it too long. Three years: first in Leicester, then in Belfast. It was harder to save than I'd thought. The good jobs went to local men. We got whatever was left. Then there was nothing left, and we were the first to be let go. By Christmas, I'd run through my savings. I spent January in a hostel. There was an incident, not my fault. I was still asked to leave. If it wasn't for Richard and the caravan, I'd be on the streets. I don't even have enough for a ticket home. I could ask Tetis. He'd come for me himself if he knew I was stuck. It'd only take one call. But I can't. I am ashamed. I don't want my grandfather knowing I've failed.

Catch yourself on, Vidas. That's Belfast-speak for 'wise up'. I'm about to cry over a tool belt. I haven't got time tonight. Frankie's waiting for me. I'll have a proper look for the tools tomorrow. For now, I grab the next-best thing: a big spoon from the sink. It's covered in the goulash Stefan made for dinner. Stefan was a chef in Poland. He got a job here, washing dishes in an American-themed diner. He was doing well until one of the local hoods complained – *local jobs for local people* – as if the locals were queuing up to scrape grease off plates for a fiver an hour. Stefan didn't have a job after that. Now, he does his best to cook for the sixteen of us on a two-ring hob. His food's not bad. Anything's better than endless Pot Noodles. I wipe the goulash off and head outside, picking my way through sleeping bodies.

Frankie is on the clifftop, waiting next to his caravan. It's dark. He doesn't see me coming. Even if it wasn't dark, Frankie still wouldn't see. He's almost completely blind. He hears, though. Frankie hears everything.

'Is that you, son?' he calls out. 'Did you get your tools?'

I wave the big spoon at him. There's no way he'll know it's not a hammer.

Frankie's standing in front of a coil of rope. 'Will this do?' he asks, nodding at it. I say it'll be grand. I don't say much around Frankie. When I do speak, I try to sound local. He thinks I'm Billy from Craig-avon. Half the men in this country are called Billy. He thinks I'm here for half-term with my kids. Frankie's a nice old man, but even nice old men can turn on you when they find out you're foreign. He'd probably call the police if he knew I was a homeless Lithuanian and there were fifteen more like me hiding in the green caravan.

The first time I bumped into Frankie, he was standing outside, smoking in the middle of the night. He said his caravan was about to fall off the cliff. He couldn't sleep for worrying it might take him with it. This is the third time we've met like this. It helps me put the night in. Mostly, Frankie talks and I listen. I don't mind. I know what it's like to have no one listening to you. I miss a lot of what he says – Frankie's from Derry; his accent's so thick he might as well be speaking another language – but I can tell I'm helping, just by listening. I feel useful with Frankie, like there's a point to me again.

I make him sit on the steps while I work. He's too frail to help and I don't want him wandering over the cliff edge. I'm supposed to be pinning his caravan down: Frankie's idea, not mine. The minute he heard I was a civil engineer – big talk, on my part – he asked for help. *I understood construction. I was the very man for the job.* I hadn't the heart to tell him there was no way to tie a caravan down. If the cliff kept crumbling, eventually it would topple over. Frankie's static was further back than most. He wasn't in any immediate danger. That empty caravan on the end, the one beside the bench they've put up for Frankie's dead daughter, is so wobbly now it'll hardly see the end of the month. I could easily have reassured him, but for one brief second I found myself wondering what Tetis would do. Before common sense could catch up with me, I heard myself saying, yes, I would help. I'd pin Frankie's caravan down. I had tools with me. It wasn't the rational thing to do, but it was kind. I can usually tell when people need kindness. It doesn't mean I'm going to give it to them.

Tetis always took the time to be kind. It used to drive me insane: the hours he'd spend listening to his workers' sob stories, the money lost covering holidays and hospital appointments, the Christmas presents for the workers' families. I told him it wasn't necessary or expected. Tetis agreed with me. He kept doing it anyway. He used to say everybody had a crack in them, a fracture running the whole way through their being. If you looked hard enough, you could always see this line. It's where a person's broken. You had a choice with people. You could use their weakness against them, or you could do your best to hold them together. Both were a form of power.

It took me about five seconds to see there was a crack running all the way through Frankie, a huge chasm of hurt. Frankie's the human version of the Grand Canyon. He's not unique. Half the people in this place are just as broken. It is a ruined sort of country. It could do with moving on. Frankie tells me his whole sad story again while I'm pretending to pin the caravan down.

As I'm tying the ropes on, I get the bit about his wife and his wee girl, Lynette; how they were happy together. *Happy as Larry* is the way he puts it (they've some funny sayings in this country). While I'm bending his coat hangers into pegs, he cries quietly, remembering the day Lynette went on ahead to wait in the car. 'A bomb,' he explains. 'We were on our holidays. I forgot to check. You always had to check back then, if you were in the RUC.' Frankie wasn't the only one who lost everything in the Troubles. It still felt like he was. His wife died shortly after. He tells me her heart was broke. By the time I'm using Stefan's big spoon to drive the pegs into the ground, he's pulled himself together. He's past the Troubles and stuck in the present, repeating the same thing he's told me these last two nights. 'Everything's gone, son.' He places his hand on the caravan. He pats it tenderly as if it is a pet dog. 'This here's the only thing left of my girls,' he says. 'I'm not for losing it too.'

I've finished now. The caravan looks ludicrous, like a giant balloon, roped loosely in place. Have I helped Frankie at all, entering into this madness? A more sensible man would probably sit down beside him and speak the truth. *This isn't going to help, Frankie. Life's just going to keep taking until you've nothing left. It's best not to fight it. You've to try and move on.* The thing is, I know he wouldn't listen. Nobody else can tell you the truth. You have to learn it for yourself. It doesn't matter where you come from – Syria or Vietnam, Klaipéda or Derry – we're all wired the same. We have to do things the hard way. Pin our caravans down in the middle of the night. Bugger off to the other side of the world. Refuse to accept help from the people who love us. Here, they talk about being *thran*.

I should be honest with Frankie. I can't even be honest with myself. Instead, I call out, 'This is my grandfather's hammer, Frankie. It never failed him once. It's just what your caravan needs.' Then, I thump Stefan's big spoon against the ground with all my strength. I thump and thump and thump, so hard; I have to believe enough for both of us. There are so many ways to break a man; so many ways to piece him back together too.

6

Alma

It'd be easy to push somebody over that cliff. It's so crumbly. You could make it look like an accident. I can think of at least three different times Agatha Christie killed somebody by shoving them off a cliff. If my iPad wasn't gone, I'd google to see if there were more. I'm raging about losing my iPad. Now I have to run my investigation the old-fashioned way. Snooping around. Observing suspects. Taking notes in my jotter. Maybe it's better like this. Poirot never looked anything up on Wikipedia or checked suspects' alibis on Facebook. If Poirot was here, he'd say, *forget the iPad, Alma. Use your leetle grey cells.* I'm doing my best. I'm watching everyone, even Mum. It's always the person you least suspect.

Weird things are happening around Seacliff. It's not just the robberies. People are acting suspiciously. I've seen strange men creeping about at night. There are noises coming out of the empty caravan. Suspicious noises. I'm on red alert. I wouldn't be surprised if somebody got murdered. Actually, I wouldn't mind a wee murder. I shouldn't say that. There's already been a murder here. Not a proper Agatha Christie one – just a bomb – but a girl got killed. Her daddy's still moping about. He's really old now. I've never seen anybody look so sad. It's wrong to want a murder. But I am so bored and we're stuck in this stupid caravan for four more days.

Agatha Christie's favourite murder weapon was poison. Most poison victims die in their sleep or keel over at the dinner table. They're all *I don't feel very well, call a doctor.* Next thing, they've face-planted into their soup. *Boring!* I prefer stabbings. You get loads of blood with a stabbing. Have you read *Murder on the Orient Express?* Spoiler alert: *everybody* kills the bad guy. *It's carnage! Blood everywhere! Totally class!* Before he left, Dad took us to see the film of it. Mum had a go at him because it was a Twelve and bits of it were about S.E.X. I don't actually think she was that bothered. It was just another thing for her to be angry about. Mum's good at getting angry with Dad. I'm kind of glad he moved to Norway. It's easier to ignore them fighting on the phone.

Mum says I've got wild morbid since Dad left. It's not healthy for a child to be obsessed with crime and murder. She's probably right. Nobody else in my class even knows who Agatha Christie is. They read baby books like *Harry Potter.* I finished *Harry Potter* when I was eight. I hate all that make-believe stuff. Monsters. Wizards. Demons. It's Mum and Dad's thing. They studied it at university. They've been stuffing it down our throats since we were wee. I like the real world better. It's way scarier.

Anyway, it's Mum's fault I got into Agatha Christie. She keeps taking me to work with her. Kids aren't supposed to be in the university library but she tells the security guard she has *childcare issues* and he lets me in. Mum doesn't give a crap what I read so long as I'm not bothering her. There's no children's section, just twelve floors of dusty grown-up books. The librarian did her best to get me reading Jane Austen. *No, thank you.* Jane Austen's full of old, poemy language: silly girls getting married and doing embroidery. I ended up in crime fiction instead. The instant I read my first page of Agatha Christie that was me sorted. There's millions of them, more than enough to keep me going till Mum finishes her research or I get to stay home alone.

Mum won't let me do anything myself. She says it's different with the twins. They're older. There's two of them. She worries about me. She thinks the divorce has made me grow up too quickly. Every time she catches me reading a murder book she says, 'What about something more your age, Alma? Roald Dahl or David Walliams?' *David Walliams! Seriously! I'm not six any more!* I give her one of my withering looks (I copied it off the TV Miss Marple: not the smiley-eyes one, the one who's like a mean Sunday-school teacher). 'You should be thankful I'm reading anything,' I say. That always shuts Mum up. Orla and Fergus haven't lifted a book in years. They're glued to their phones, Whats-Apping their stupid mates from school. At least they

were, until their mobiles got nicked. I'd laugh, if somebody hadn't lifted my iPad too.

I've made missing posters and stuck them up around
the caravan park. I did them all by hand. The drawings
got a bit wobbly so I asked Pete if I could use his
photocopier. 'My photocopier's on the blink,' he said.
'My secretary's looking into it right after she fixes my
jacuzzi.' He was being sarcastic. Adults think kids
don't understand sarcasm. They do. I do, anyway.
Mum says I'm precocious. Dad says I'm just well read.
I don't think Pete's in any position to be making jokes.
A crime wave's happening under his nose and what's
he doing about it? Absolutely nothing. He just loafs
around his caravan looking sad and doing his music.
Every time I walk past, I can hear him playing his guitar
and singing the sort of songs Dad used to play in the
car. Whiney, old-man songs. Probably Coldplay. At
least my dad had a decent voice.

If Pete was in an Agatha Christie, he'd be the bum-
bling policeman, the one who follows the wrong lead.
He'd be no help with my investigation, so I'm not for
telling him any of the suspicious things I've seen. He
wouldn't listen anyway. Pete thinks I'm just a silly wee
girl, whingeing about her missing iPad. Good. That's
part of my plan; another thing I learnt from Miss
Marple. She pretends to be a batty old woman, so
people don't notice her snooping about. Then, boom!
She goes and cracks the case while the police are off
on another wild-goose chase. I'm like Miss Marple. I'm
working undercover, lulling the thief into a false sense
of security. I've got the best disguise ever. Nobody

pays any attention to wee girls. I'm aiming to have this case solved before half-term's over. Ideally, a bit sooner. I've a load of homework to get done before school starts again.

Pete said I could add his missing documents to my posters, though really there wasn't any point. He can easily get another set printed. He just has to ask his uncle. You'd think he'd be pleased about this, but he actually looked disappointed, like Mum does every time she gets off the phone with Dad. I asked him what was in the documents. He told me to mind my own business. I'm used to suspects withholding information. You can't force them to talk when you're not the police. I don't feel sorry for Pete, even though he looks miserable. He's still on my suspects list. He could've stolen his own documents to draw suspicion away from himself. In Agatha Christie, people are always murdering people they don't have to, just to throw Poirot off the scent. I have to stay alert. Trust no one.

The clock's ticking. I've only got a few days left. I don't feel the investigation's getting anywhere. This morning, I stuck more posters up all over the campsite. I even sellotaped one to the empty caravan, though nobody's supposed to be up there. Pete's covered it in red warning signs. *Danger. Subsidence.* Any day now, that caravan's going to slide over the cliff. I tiptoed round the sides, peeking through the closed curtains. I couldn't see anything inside or get in to investigate. There was an enormous padlock on the door and stripy tape running round the walls. It looked like a wrapped-up Christmas present. It's obvious no one's been inside since I began staking it out, but when I placed my ear against the door and listened really hard, I swear I could hear something scrabbling about. For a second I wondered if it might be a ghost. Then I reminded myself that detectives do not believe in ghosts. We're talking basic rules of deduction here: *there's a logical reason for everything*. Still, I should probably tell Pete about the noises. Technically, he's in charge. He'd just try to convince me it's a rat or a really big spider. He's not a detective. He doesn't have intuition like me. I know there's something going on in that caravan. I'm going to get to the bottom of it.

Other people have started adding their own missing items to my posters. A briefcase. Maggie the dog. A tool belt. Golf clubs. Jamie Oliver's *30-Minute Meals*. A fountain pen. Sixty-four handwritten letters. The Queen, in a nice silver frame. At the bottom of one of them somebody's written, *I'll give twenty pounds for the return of my big Thermos flask*, and added their phone number. The list makes no sense. It's just a load of random crap. There must be something linking the stolen items, but I can't figure out what it is. Do they have some kind of value I'm not seeing? Maybe they mean something special to their owners. What's the thief planning to do with them?

I'm back in our caravan now, working on the case. Mum's gone off hunting sea monsters (don't even ask). The twins have cycled into Ballycastle to see if the library's got the Internet. I'm at the table, building a house of cards. This is what Poirot does when he's concentrating. Obviously, Poirot wouldn't use Star Wars

Top Trumps, but I can't find anything else. I do my best not to wobble. I line the cards up edge to edge: Princess Leia on Darth Vader. I'm giving my brain some space to think. The key to cracking a case is logic; logic and concentration. Once you know why a crime's been committed, it's dead easy to work out who did it. *Think hard, Alma. What do the stolen items mean?* I wish I was more like Poirot. All this sitting around thinking's dead boring. It feels more like maths than detective work. If I could, I'd skip forwards to the part where the case gets solved and everybody sees how clever I am.

The big reveal is my favourite part of Agatha Christie. I know exactly how I'm going to do mine. I don't have a library to gather the suspects in, but Seacliff's rec room will do rightly. I'll make everybody sit in a circle on foldy chairs. Pete. Mum. Fergus and Orla. All the people from the caravans. Maybe I'll give them orange squash or wine to keep them from leaving. Then, I'll stand in the middle and say, 'You're all gathered here this evening because one of you is a dirty thief.' There'll be lots of gasps and maybe some swearing. Hopefully, at least one person will faint. I'll take ages to explain how I solved the case. I won't say who done it till the very last second. The thief will be sitting there, squirming in their foldy chair. I'll have the police waiting outside. Even though they've been absolutely useless, I'll need them when I do the big reveal. Sometimes the criminal makes a run for it, and I don't have a gun to shoot them with. Everybody will be dead impressed. They'll say things like, 'I didn't realize you had it in you, Alma.' I'll probably get on the TV news. Not the real news, just the Northern Ireland one. It'd still be class, though, being on TV.

I place Luke Skywalker carefully on top of my stack. My hand wobbles as I settle him into position and the whole house of cards slowly topples. Cards might work for Poirot but they're not doing anything for me. I reach for my backpack. I'll go through the clues one more time before the twins come back and pester me. My bag's not as heavy as it should be. I know what's happened straight away. I'm not even surprised. The thief has struck again. This time it's my jotter. Seriously, how am I meant to solve this case when everything keeps disappearing? And how did the thief get into my backpack? It hasn't been out of my sight all day. *Use your logic, Alma.* If a crime has happened under your nose and you haven't seen anything, then the criminal must be invisible. *Invisible thief.* I write this down on the back of an envelope. I haven't a baldy clue what it means.

Sometimes I wish real life was more like an Agatha Christie. Half the bad things that happen don't make any sense. Big things like Donald Trump and the icebergs melting. Small things too, like my stolen stuff and Dad leaving and Martha in the caravan next door. She doesn't know who she is any more. I feel sad for her and John. There's something about Seacliff that makes me feel sad. I suspect it isn't just me. Nobody here seems properly happy. I don't understand why they keep coming if it makes them so miserable. Maybe it isn't Seacliff. Maybe they bring the sadness here. If you're not careful, sadness can get stuck to you. I don't know how to help them. Sadness isn't like crime or murder. Sad stuff just happens. You can't blame anybody for it. You can't solve it either. And if you can't solve a problem, how do you make it go away? I'm doing my best here, but I'm not Poirot. I'm just Alma and I'm stuck too.

7

Malcolm

Today is the first day of the rest of my life. It was going to be yesterday, then Susan dropped in to see how I was getting on and, well, it was pretty obvious I wasn't. It was two in the afternoon. I was still in my pyjamas. We had words. Loud words. Arguing in a caravan's the same as arguing in a tent. Every nosy bugger can hear you. You should've seen the look that young fella gave me; the poncey one in the flashy suit. Me and Susan were having a slanging match on the steps when he came out of the green caravan. He looked right down his snobby nose at us. Now, Susan was fairly screaming at that stage, 'Where is it, Malcolm? You're reeking of it.' She didn't believe it was last night's drink she'd got a whiff of. I was a different fella now.

Susan never found my stash. You'd think after fifteen years she'd know all my tricks. I've my cans hidden under the caravan. I'd every intention of dumping them yesterday. I never did. By the time she left I was gagging. The woman drove me to it. One can led to another. I can't remember anything after six. But today's a new day, as they say in the movies. I'm never touching another drop.

I'm off to a tremendous start. Up at eight. Half an hour of Susan's mindfulness tape. She's got me into all that New Age shite. It's supposed to centre me. A sneaky bowl of Coco Pops. Then, a dander along the cliff to get the cobwebs shifted. I see that's where they've dumped the dead girl's bench. It's a view and a half, but you wouldn't want to be up there after you've had a few. The whole thing's sliding and it's sixty feet down to the beach. Any day now, that empty caravan on the end'll be going for an impromptu paddle. It wouldn't take much to move it back. If I was in shape, I'd have a go myself. I've shifted bigger: Da's combine harvester, them boats for Uncle Sammy, our Ellen's Micra when it got stuck in the ditch.

I can't lift shit these days. The thing with Lewis has got to me. I've let myself go. Susan's probably right. I have been going a bit hard on the drink. That's why I'm down here, taking the lend of Marty McClintock's caravan. They say a change is as good as a rest. This place'll help me get back on form. If I was on top form I'd be just as big as Lewis, maybe bigger. Granted, I don't have his good looks. Lewis takes after our ma. I got Da's ugly bake. But, I'm every bit as strong as him and I scrub up rightly when I make the effort. Decent haircut and a shave. New suit. Susan says I lose two stone in a suit. Wait till you see,

I'll be on the telly before Christmas. I just need to get my head together.

I'm starting small and building up. I could probably manage a tin of beans or a couple of saucepans. But it's been such a long time since I tried to lift anything, I'll go easy on myself. I'm beginning with the first thing Da taught me to lift; the first thing his da taught him. I was six, the morning he sat me down in front of a teaspoon and showed me how to raise it up in the air. 'If you get the technique right, son, there's nothing you can't turn your mind to.' After that, there was no stopping me; I was levitating Da's prize heifers by the end of the week.

It's not coming easy this morning. There's something about this place. Everything feels heavier here. Maybe it's because of that girl who died. A murder leaves something hanging in the air. It's a scientific fact. They had it on *The X-Files* once. I've been staring at this teaspoon for an hour. It hasn't budged an inch. It's not even wobbled. You need a clean head to lift and mine's pure thumping from last night's session. I'll hardly be making much progress today, but I can't give up. Every time I think about calling it a day – maybe cracking open a wee can to ease the head – I remember the billboard opposite the chipper. Forty friggin' feet of my brother's big lardy face taunting me every time I go in for a fish supper. *Luke LaGuardia, the next generation's David Blaine.*

Folks stop me in the street to ask, 'Is that not your Lewis in the purple satin get-up? He's done well for himself with the magic. Why's he going by a different

name?' *Why indeed? What the hell's wrong with plain
old Lewis Leckey?* He says it doesn't have the same ring
to it. They made him change it for the TV show. He
had to learn how to speak better too. Apparently, English ones aren't great with provincial accents. It's
mostly English folk who watch that show. Whatever
they done, it worked. My brother's a big cheese now.
He's got his own programme starting soon and a sta-
dium tour. Next year Comic Relief are getting him to
lift Blackpool Tower. He claims he wanted to do Stormont, but his agent thought there might be political
connotations.

It's just big talk on Lewis's part. Shifting Stormont.
Doing his PR photos at the Giant's Causeway. Inviting
Liam Neeson on to his show like the pair of them were
old muckers. My brother's only from here when it suits
him. The truth is, he sold out long ago. He's forgotten
where he came from. Maybe he's ashamed of it. He's
only acting the local celebrity now he's famous. The
same boy couldn't get away from here quick enough.
You shouldn't pretend to be something you're not. I
don't care how fed up you are.

When I get my break, I won't be flaffing around in
a sequined jumpsuit or speaking all *la-di-dah.* I won't
be relocating to bloody Kent. Would I consider chan-
ging my name? I would not. I'm proud to be Cully-
backey born and bred, proud to have cut my teeth
lifting tractors on a farm. Damn it, I'm even proud to
sound like I've a mouthful of boiled potatoes. I'll be
prouder still when I've my own billboard. *Malcolm
Leckey, Ulster's premier telekineticist.* (I'd have a wee

note at the bottom explaining telekinetics is moving stuff with your mind, in case folks thought it was something to do with fixing phones.)

I'm well into my second hour working on the teaspoon when somebody gives the door a clatter. It's the girl with the yellow wellies. The staring one. She's going door to door like a Born Again, asking people if they're missing anything. Apparently, Seacliff's in the middle of a crime wave. She's *trying to establish a motive for the crimes*. I'm not kidding. Them's her actual words. She's Inspector Morse reincarnated. I could see her far enough.

'Aren't you a bit young for the police?' I say. 'The PSNI's not what it used to be.'

She doesn't even crack a smile, just keeps right on interrogating me.

I tell her I've not lost anything.

'Would you notice if you had?' she asks.

Cheeky wee bugger. I've had nothing stronger than Punjana this morning, though maybe she can smell last night's drink. In fairness, the whole caravan's stinking of it. Still, I hate the way she's glaring at me. The wean's five foot nothing, yet she's managing to look down on me. Susan's got a knack of doing the very same thing. I'd call it a gift – *I lift things, she shrinks them* – but it's nothing special. Every woman I know can make you feel *that high*, just by looking at you the right way.

I bet our Lewis is clean pestered with wee blades like this, demanding autographs and selfies. Nobody's looking down on him these days. Just thinking about

Lewis makes me angry. I can feel the hot rage building up behind my eyes. It's not a bad feeling. You can take the energy and channel it. Susan would call it mindfulness. Bollocks. It's just taking your anger out on the right thing. First time a girl turned me down, I went out of that disco and lifted two parked cars. The day Lewis got on the telly, I shifted our garage, ten feet down the lane, then brought it back when Susan started giving off. I can feel it coming on me now. I'm that angry, I could make mincemeat of the teaspoon. I could lift a table, or an armchair, maybe even the whole caravan. I haven't got a live TV audience, but I do have this lassie in her yellow wellies. I'd like to wipe that smug look off her face.

'Here,' I say. 'Do you want to see a magic trick? Come in and I'll show you.'

I'll probably just lift some cutlery for her. I wouldn't want to look like I was showing off.

The child goes a funny colour. All the bluster's gone out of her. She looks much younger than before. She starts backing away.

'I can lift things with my mind,' I say. 'Just come in a minute till you see.' I'm aware that I sound like a paedo but I can't seem to stop myself. I don't want her to think bad of me. I want her to like me. I want everybody to like me. Susan says that's my biggest problem. It doesn't matter what I do. I'm not a very likeable man.

The girl's turning away now. I've freaked her out. She looks back over her shoulder as she leaves. 'They taught us about men like you in school,' she says. 'Stranger danger and all that. I'm for telling my mum you tried to get me into your caravan. And Pete. And probably the police too.' She runs a few feet, then stops, turns and gives me the finger. It's meant to be defiant. It just looks pathetic. 'I'm putting you at the top of my suspects list!' she shouts, then disappears into her caravan.

I go back inside and close the door. I'll have to go and find the caretaker before she gets to him. I'll end up telling him about Lewis. People always look sceptical when I talk about my gift. They nod and give me that patronizing look. They think I'm not all there. The instant I say, 'Do you know Luke LaGuardia? He's my brother, so he is,' the whole situation changes. 'Oh,' they say, 'you mean you're an illusionist.' It's simpler just to pretend I am.

It's still the first day of the rest of my life but I'm going to have one wee drink to steady my nerves. I fish the bottle of Bushmills out from behind the fridge. I can't believe Susan didn't find it. She's getting sloppy. She's miles away, back home, but I can't help feeling guilty. I swear I can feel her staring at me. I have a wee nip. Then a second. The teaspoon's still sitting there, taunting me. I'm not in the mood for trying again. That wee girl has pissed me off. I put it back in the cutlery drawer. Tomorrow's a new day, as they say in the movies. I'll get up early. I'll do a whole hour of mindfulness. Hell, I'll do some yoga on the dead girl's bench. I'll have the spoon up before lunchtime. It'll be just like that cartoon with Mickey Mouse: spoons and plates flying everywhere. *Here now*, I think, *a stunt like that would look class on the telly if I done it right.*

I pour myself a mug of whiskey, then a second mug. I forget all about the caretaker. I fall asleep on the sofa and dream a brilliant dream. Here's me, doing the *Royal Variety*. There's Lizzie and Big Philip in the front row, Ant and Dec in the wings cheering me on. Out I come in my shiny grey suit to rapturous applause. I don't even bother with the build-up. I just lift Lewis up into the gods and drop him on his big, fat head.

When I wake, it's dark. Two yellow headlights sweep through the caravan, cutting the night in two. A car pulls up next door. I crawl over to the window to watch. A young woman is unpacking the boot, carting stuff up the path into the caravan. I can tell she has a baby. She's got all the paraphernalia with her. Sure enough, the last thing out of the car's a wee pink blob in a carry seat. She sets it on the tarmac for a second, while she locks the car.

I stare at the baby. It glows under the security light like Baby Jesus in Catholic paintings. It stares at me like it's seeing right through me. Sometimes babies don't look like babies. They look like adults trapped in baby faces. They freak me out. They're only wee but they can still make you feel crap. It's like they know who you really are. I'm concentrating so hard on staring down the baby I make its carry seat lift half a foot up in the air. It's dark. I've been drinking. I haven't lifted anything in months. But I know exactly what I've done. I've still got it. *Yeooooo!* Tomorrow's a new day, as they say in the movies. I'll begin my comeback in the morning. Tonight, I'm celebrating. I go out to grab some cans from under the caravan, but they're gone. Every bleeding one of them. Crime wave or not, I blame that wee girl.

8

Kathleen

Where does all this dust come from? I cleaned when we got here and the caravan's pigging again already. I always give it a good going-over in February. It gets fusty over the winter. I was especially careful, with the baby coming and everything. When mine were wee, you didn't worry about dirt. A bit of dirt hardened a wean. Things are different now. They have that child wrapped in cotton wool. Everything has to be sterilized and organic and vegan. Poor wee mite. The way they're getting on, he won't be allowed outside till he's twenty.

I blame that woman. She's Australian (among other things). Claudia; I'll give her her name but I'm not for calling her Melanie's wife because there's no such thing. You can't have two women married to each other. It isn't right. The Bible says so. I have been civil with her. It's the Christian thing to do. Trevor says you should hate the sin and love the sinner, though there's no love lost between the two of them. He didn't want Claudia down here this weekend. 'Just family,' he said, 'like old times.' Course he couldn't tell Melanie this himself. I had to make the awkward phone call; there's nobody in Ulster does more for peace and reconciliation than me. I've no choice. I don't want to lose Melanie or Max. He's our first grandbaby. Wee dote; I'd be heartbroken if I didn't get to see him. Thankfully, the weekend sorted itself out. Claudia's at a conference. She couldn't come even if we'd wanted her.

I was hoping to take Max out for a dander this morning. Truth be told, I was planning to show him off. We've been coming to Seacliff so long we know all the regulars. Anna. Poor old Frankie. Lois and her troop (dear love her, struggling on by herself). John and Martha across the way. It's them we'd be closest to. We used to share lifts into church on Sundays. It's a shame about Martha. I hadn't seen her since September. She's gone downhill so quickly. I thought a cuddle with Max might lift her. Babies are good for people with Alzheimer's. They help them remember. I'll go round with him tomorrow instead. Probably best not to take the child round to Frankie's. He's in a wild state this week, it being Lynette's big birthday. I wouldn't want to rub it in. I mean, our situation's not ideal, but at least our girl's still around.

The whole morning's going to be taken up with cleaning now Trevor's landed this on me. 'Oh, by the way,' he says, casual as you like, before breakfast, 'the minister's calling round later. To have a word with Melanie.' There's no point asking if Melanie knows she's getting a papal visit. She'd be halfway home already if she knew. No, this is entirely her father's doing, a typical Trevor manoeuvre. I almost told him to catch himself on. Could we not just have one nice weekend together, pretending to be normal? It was right there on the tip of my tongue. But I didn't say anything. I just got my duster out for the minister. I'm not scared of Trevor. I just know my place. He's the head of the house. It doesn't matter what I think. I've to do what he says. The Bible says so.

Melanie's gone for a jog. She's getting back in shape. I think it's a bit soon myself. When I had her, they kept me in hospital a full week. Claudia's big into her fitness. It's the Australian thing. You should see the stuff she eats. It looks like what you'd feed a cat. She had Melanie doing yoga right up to the birth. Now, she's out running. Obviously, we're not keen on the yoga. It's a bit New Age-y; not as bad as out-and-out satanism, but not to be dabbled with either. And it can't be good for her, having all her bits jiggled about so soon after the baby. But I didn't say anything when she put the runners on this morning. I've learnt to pick my battles. 'Enjoy your run, love,' I said. 'Be careful on that cliff.' It was nice to get some Nanny time with Max.

Trevor's away to the shops. I can't be offering the minister plain digestives and there's nothing else in the cupboards. I've given all my traybakes to Frankie. I was trying to cheer him up. It's just me and the wee man this morning. He's propped up in his carry seat watching me dust. I'm singing away. *Jesus wants me for a sunbeam.* Melanie's asked me not to indoctrinate the child. What she doesn't know won't hurt her. I'm thinking of his eternal soul. Claudia would be raging if she heard me. She'd probably call the NSPCC. She's made it abundantly clear Max won't be brought up *religious*. No Sunday-school choruses. No bedtime prayers. Obviously, no baptism (I don't even think the minister's allowed to do babies like Max in our church).

If I think about it too much, I get weepy. Me and Trevor haven't told anybody about Melanie, only the minister, and you have to tell ministers things like this. Our church friends know we have a grandbaby we can't bring out on a Sunday morning. We told them Melanie was backslidden. They understood that. Lots of their own weans never darken the door of a church. I wanted to tell Mike and Sally the truth; Mike and Sally are our oldest friends. They'd understand. But Trevor wouldn't let me. There's no way he's for telling anybody our daughter is living with another woman. He can't even say the words himself. How could he possibly admit it to anybody else? We let people think Melanie's just ordinary backslidden. There's less shame in it.

I move Max from the table to the sofa so I can get at the blinds. They're a right dust trap. As I drag the cloth across the window, the morning light comes streaming through and lands on his face. He's lit up like an angel. I know I'm biased but Max is one bonny-looking baby. He's the spit of his mummy at that age. I used to sing the same choruses to her. *He made the stars to shine. Jesus's love is very wonderful.* Even when she was a tiny scrap of a thing, she'd make noises like she was singing along. My mother, Melanie's granny, used to say the joy of the Lord was clean shining out of her. You wouldn't have known there was anything wrong with the child. Maybe there wasn't back then. Maybe we're to blame for the way she's turned out. I think about this a lot. Could we have done anything differently?

The minister says everybody's born in sin. The Bible says so. It's hard to see it, when you look at wee Max. Sure, he looks perfect, doesn't he? Look at that face. I'd never say this to Trevor, but sometimes I think the same thing about Melanie. Even now. I look at her and she still seems perfect to me. I don't know how to love her less. I know I should. I should be taking every opportunity to tell her where she's gone wrong. It's not too late. Anybody can repent and Jesus'll forgive them, even murderers. I should be sitting Melanie down and telling her what she's doing with Claudia is wrong. I just can't seem to get the words out. It's hard, so it is, hurting your child on purpose.

I'm getting myself into a state just thinking about it. I put down the duster and lift Max out of his seat. It's not just ones with Alzheimer's that benefit from baby cuddles. I dandle him on my knee. *Who's Nanny's best boy?* He gurgles back and reaches to rub my face. I could eat him with a spoon. 'Come here till I show you something, Maxi,' I say, scooching up the sofa till we're next to the cabinet where I keep my treasures. Mammy's Royal Doulton. Our wedding photo. The twenty-third psalm done in cross-stitch. (We got that on a mission trip to Tanzania.)

I lift down the framed photo of Melanie and Jamesy Thompson. I wipe the dust off the glass. It hurts to look at it for too long. My beautiful daughter. Her handsome boyfriend. Off to the school formal in their fancy outfits. 'That's your mummy,' I say, pointing Melanie out to Max. 'Isn't she beautiful, like a princess? Doesn't she look happy?' Even as I'm speaking, I'm wondering if she was happy. Would I have noticed if she wasn't? I put the photo back on the shelf, angling it in behind an ornament. If Melanie spots it, she'll have a pink fit. I'm just not ready to throw it out yet. It's my favourite photo of her.

I lift Max up to look out the window. I point out the birdies on the fence and the sea beyond. Lois's youngest is stomping about in those wild-looking yellow wellies. She's a strange child, Alma; very intense. She's never done asking questions. Lois says the first word out of her was *why?* She's joking, though it wouldn't surprise me. It drives Trevor mad the way Lois answers all her questions. She talks to her weans like they're adults. When she split up with the husband, Alma was fit to tell me the ins and outs of the whole divorce. She was only ten. You have to protect a child that age. They're not old enough to know everything. Still, I have to say I envy them – calearied as they are – at least they talk to each other, really properly talk. We're all adults in this caravan but we'll spend the whole weekend talking about nothing. The weather. The baby. Whether or not to put the kettle on. Avoiding the elephant in the room because nobody wants to cause a scene.

At least, that's how it's always been. Even before Claudia appeared. Back home there was space to avoid each other. The caravan felt different. We had to tip-toe round each other here. We couldn't risk looking each other in the eye. This weekend is going to be different. There'll be no going back to normal after the minister wades in. Our Melanie's easy-going but she'll not sit there quietly, sipping her tea while a stranger tells her she's living in sin. Why should she? She's made it quite clear she isn't religious any more. I can't believe Trevor's doing this. It's the baby. Max has tipped him over the edge. When it was just her and Claudia he could tell himself they were only friends, two girls sharing a flat together. When Max came along, and Claudia insisted they get married, he couldn't pretend any longer. There was no getting round what our daughter had become. A lesbian. There, I said it. Doesn't mean I have to like it. But you've to be honest about these things, don't you? Honesty's in the Bible too.

Max begins to gurn. I carry him into the kitchen to fix a bottle. While the kettle boils, I slip my finger into his wee mouth to calm him. Melanie doesn't believe in dummies. Max sucks at my finger greedily. He looks up at me with his big blue eyes. Nobody in our family has blue eyes. Dear only knows where he got them from. I don't even want to ask. I was so scared I wouldn't love him. When Melanie told me, it was the first thing I thought of. I didn't want a grandbaby this way. I wanted my daughter properly married to a nice fella – somebody like Jamesy Thompson – before the weans started appearing. I'd be one of those proud grannies, showing my grandson off round everybody in church. I thought I'd have to pretend to like the child, knowing how he got made. I wasn't expecting to love him this much. It's almost painful. It's like some part of me's missing when he isn't around.

It's the same with Melanie. I can't stop loving her. I can't see past the love. I should be stronger. Some would say I should cut her out altogether. For her own good. I should be on Trevor's side, sitting next to him, nodding along when the minister tries to talk sense into her. But I'm not. I can't. It's more than a feeling. It's a physical thing. The hard words won't come. See, a mother's bent towards protecting her children. I'm not capable of hurting Melanie. At least not on purpose.

I make a decision. Before I can change my mind, I fish out my mobile and text the minister. I don't have the guts to call. I'm scared he'll hear I'm lying. I type one-handed, with Max squirming in my arms. *Sorry. Have to cancel. Baby's sick.* The lie comes easier than I'd expected. Maybe I'm backsliding too. I carry Max and his bottle over to the sofa. If the minister's not coming, I've the afternoon free. I could take the baby round the caravans to meet everybody. Melanie could come along. She'd like that. I'd like it too. I glance out the window to see if John and Martha are in. My eye lights upon the cabinet. There's a gap behind my ornaments. Melanie's formal photo has disappeared. I'm not into signs or anything, but I wonder if this is some kind of message from the Lord. Maybe it's time to think about moving on. I probably should've got rid of it years ago. I wish it was that simple. It isn't. None of this is. I turn the place upside down, looking for my photo. By the time Trevor gets back, I've worked myself up into a state.

9

John

I must look unhinged: an old man, wandering around a caravan park in pyjamas. You'd think it was me doting, not Martha. The rain isn't helping. I'm soaked to the skin. Now the shock's wearing off, I'm only just noticing how cold I am. You can probably hear my teeth chattering from the far side of Ballycastle. Maybe Pete'll lend me a jumper. I give his caravan door another rattle. It's four in the morning. Everybody's trying to sleep. I'm the last person to cause a scene, but this is an emergency. My girl's gone missing. I'll raise the whole site if I have to.

I shouldn't have brought her here. Paula at the memory clinic said it might help to talk about the past. Like an eejit, I thought I'd do one better. I'd bring Martha down to the caravan. It'd give her a wee lift; remind her of all the good times we had. Paula also said, *don't make any drastic changes to Martha's routine.* Muggins here thought he knew better. Sure, the

sea air's meant to be a tonic. They're always taking
invalids to the coast in Jane Austen. I should've run my
plans past Paula, because Martha's not just remembering the past. She's been stuck in it since we got here,
going on and on about taking the girls to the sea, acting like we're back in 1983. *Where's Jenny? Have I seen
Sandra's swimsuit? What about going for a paddle?* It's
like a broken record. It never stops. Something about
this place is playing on her. I've tried every trick in the
book – distractions, reasoning with her, entering into
her daft delusions – poor Martha's still trapped in the
last happy summer at Seacliff. The year before Lynette.

   She's been so confused since Christmas. Sometimes
she doesn't even know who I am. On good days she
takes me for her brother. I can deal with that. She was
fond of him. On bad days, I'm a stranger. Once, she
called the police on me. Can you believe that? My own
wife of fifty-odd years, ringing 999 because I scared
her. Mostly she just shouts. Paula says there's no point
trying to reason with her; distraction's more likely to
work. I go out, walk around the block and, when I
come back, she's usually herself again, all eager to tell
me about the bad man who was sitting in my chair.

   She hit me once. Only once, with a soup ladle. It
was an accident. I kept my sleeves down till the bruise
faded. I didn't bother telling the girls. They'd only
have used it against me. They mean the best, but sometimes I could see the pair of them far enough. Every
other day, I get the whole spiel: *it's time to reconsider
your options, Dad. For Mum's sake as well as your own.* As
far as I'm concerned, there's no options to reconsider.

I can look after my own wife rightly. No nursing home. No strangers coming in to bath her and dress her. Martha would be mortified. She's always been a very private lady.

I can hear Pete stirring. I give the door one last clatter. We need to get moving. Martha could be miles away already. She's done this before, at home. While I was in the shower, she managed to make it halfway into town. One of the neighbours brought her back. She was in her pyjamas. I'm exhausted looking after her. It's not just tonight. It's been like this for ages. I lean against the door and try to steady myself. I'm still woozy from the tablets. I probably shouldn't have taken them, but I was desperate for a decent night's sleep. Martha's been so restless. Up and down to the loo, every twenty minutes. Shuffling round the caravan, making piles of stuff on the floor. I caught her in the girls' old room two nights ago, sitting on Jenny's bed, reading to her as if she was actually there. It wasn't even a real story: bits of *The Water-Babies* – that used to be the girls' favourite – and Bible verses and a lot of nonsense talk.

I'm ashamed to say she wore me down. There's only so many times you can say, 'Come back to bed, pet,' before you lose your temper. I'm not the best when I'm tired. So, this evening, I gave her a sleeping tablet along with her pills. I took one myself and wondered why I hadn't thought of it before. Now I know. The tablet did nothing for Martha. I slept so hard I didn't notice she'd gone. She left the caravan door wide open, rattling in the wind – that didn't even wake me. Of all the nights to do a runner. It's wild out there. The rain's coming down in sheets. She'll be petrified, poor love. She hasn't even got her slippers on.

I raise my fist but Pete's already opening the door. 'What the hell?' he mutters. 'It's the middle of the night.' He looks worse than me. Bleary-eyed. Unshaven. Like a bear that's been hibernating. I can smell the drink on him. 'It's Martha,' I mumble. 'I can't find her.' Pete sobers up quick sharp. He's not half the caretaker his Uncle Jim was, but I can tell he's doing his best. He asks sensible questions. *When did I last see Martha? What's she wearing? Has she done this sort of thing before?* I'm no use at all. I start to cry. I'm not a weepy man. I haven't cried since my mother's funeral but here I am, standing on his doorstep bawling like a wean. Pete's good about it. He hands me a wad of kitchen roll. 'You've had a shock,' he says. He brings me inside, shifting the clutter from his sofa so I can sit. He gives me a nip of whiskey to warm me. I'm not used to the whiskey. It burns my throat and makes my nose run. I can feel the tears coming again. Pete pretends not to notice. He calls 999 and asks for police and ambulance. He glances out the window, at the rain lashing across the clifftop. 'Maybe let the coastguard know as well,' he says. He fishes two torches out of the kitchen drawer and we go off to round up a search party.

People are awful kind. Even strangers. You don't realize how kind they are until you're in the middle of a crisis. Not one person complains about being woken up in the middle of the night. They all say the same thing: 'I'm coming now, just let me grab a coat.' Course, I expected our friends to help. Anna. Lois. Frankie. The Fletchers: we've known Kathleen and Trevor for thirty years, ever since we started coming to Seacliff. Their wee ones grew up with ours. If things had been different, the next generation would've been doing the same. Racing their bikes and playing football on the green. It won't be like that now. However tonight turns out, this'll be our last time at the caravan. Kathleen called round this morning with her new grandson in tow. It was kind of her. For a while it lifted Martha. She remembered what to do with a baby. She had him cradled in her arms, talking baby talk. Wee Max played along, gurgling and smiling up at her. Martha hadn't been that content in ages. She looked like herself again.

Then, something changed. I've seen it happen so many times now, but the change still shocks me. It's like watching the sky cloud over before a storm. Martha's face fell. Her whole body tightened. She started talking gobbledygook about babies and swimming and water. Before I could stop her, she was up and across the room. She'd the kitchen tap going full blast and Max held under it, screaming. Kathleen was really nice about it. She said there was no harm done. She even made a joke of it, *sure, wasn't it about time the child was properly baptized?* I tried to laugh. I couldn't. I was mortified. And also scared. I knew what Martha was up to. Paula in the memory clinic's warned me about this. Sometimes people living with dementia can't tell the difference between reality and made-up stuff. They'll

talk about things in films or on TV as if they really happened. Even books can confuse them. I should've seen
this coming. Martha's been carrying around Jenny's
old copy of *The Water-Babies* since we got here. She
keeps asking when we're for taking the children down
to the sea. 'It's nice in the water,' she says. 'It's better
there.'

Pete and I make our way from one end of the site to
the other, battering on doors and explaining what's
happened. People I've never seen before come stum-
bling out of their caravans, half asleep. A big beefy fella
in a tracksuit emerges from Marty McClintock's and
offers to help. Much use he'll be. He's four sheets to
the wind. He can barely stand up. The green caravan's
a better bet. It takes a few minutes to rouse the occu-
pants, but when they start piling out, I can't believe
how many there are. Pete looks equally bemused.
There's a dozen fellas or more inside. Dear only knows
who they are, for they're clearly not related. Most of
them are foreign. Half don't even speak English. Maybe
they're here on a stag weekend. We're plagued with
stag weekends at the minute. It's the cheap flights that
attract them. Listen, those lads could be drug-dealing
terrorists for all I care. I'm glad to have them on board.
The more people out looking, the better chance we
have of finding her.

I should speak to these folk myself, but I'm too jit-
tery. I stand next to Pete while he explains what's happened. Lois's wee one pipes up from the back. 'Do you
think Martha's been stolen, like all the other things? I
think the thief's nicking things that mean a lot to

people. John always says Martha means the world to him.' God love the child. I'm off again. Bawling my eyes out. Lois takes Alma aside. I can hear her explaining gently that Martha's poorly in her head and she sometimes gets confused about what is real. Alma looks at her mother like she's the mad one. 'Do you mean she has dementia, Mum?' she asks. That child's old before her time. She knows far too much.

A fella in a blue jumper elbows his way to the front. He's one of the green-caravan contingent. He doesn't look foreign but when he speaks you can tell he's not from here. 'Please,' he says urgently, 'the lady is gone in the sea.' A ripple of alarm runs round the crowd. He corrects himself quickly. 'Sorry, my English is not good. The lady is *going* to the sea.' I know he's right. I don't need to hear his story. The way he met Martha two nights ago, sitting on the memorial bench with a children's book clutched in her hands. How she'd been reading aloud to nobody but insisted the story was for Lynette. How she'd told this man he looked sad in his eyes, like he wanted to be somewhere else, and he'd admitted she was right: there was nothing for him in this place. How she'd pointed at the book and said, *it's all in here, son. You can have a better life, under the water.* The way he'd been scared for her, so close to the cliff edge, in nothing but her nightdress, and led her back to her own caravan and would have – *no, should have* – told someone, if he hadn't been so scared and selfish, only thinking of himself.

I let the lad say his piece. I know he's telling the truth. I know it in my guts. The same way I know my

Martha's never coming back to me. Oh, we might find her this evening, shivering in a ditch or trying to pick her way down the path to the beach. We might well find her, but she won't be my Martha any more. She hasn't been my Martha for a long time now. For the smallest, ugliest moment, I wonder if it might be better not to find her. Would it be the worst thing in the world to let her go? She might be right. Maybe she would be happier under the sea. I don't have time to dwell on this thought. Pete is rallying the troops, instructing us to spread out along the cliff edge. We'll sweep our way forwards, calling out for Martha as we go. 'She can't have got very far,' says Kathleen, hooking her arm through mine.

We're barely two minutes into the search when the shout goes up. It comes echoing along the line. *Over here. Come and help.* My heart leaps up my throat. I feel dizzy with relief. Kathleen gives my arm a squeeze, as if to say, *there you go. Everything's grand.* But it isn't Martha they've found. It's the end caravan; the old, empty one. The storm's hit the cliff hard. Huge chunks of soft ground are crumbling into the sea. The caravan's hanging over the edge, a good third of it tottering like a half-raised drawbridge. I'm inclined to let it fall – we've bigger things to worry about – until young Alma shouts out, 'You've got to stop it from falling! There's something inside. Something moving around. Do you think it could be Martha in there?'

10

Lynette

It was the bench that tipped me over. I've been here in Seacliff all along: thirty-five long years. I've been bored to the back teeth but I always kept my distance. Everything changed when Dad bought the bench. I knew I had to intervene. The caravan was bad enough. It kept him tied to this godawful place. Once that bench went up – with my name on it – he'd never leave. At first, I was only thinking of Dad. I'd give him a push in the right direction. Maybe if he finally left Seacliff, I might get to move on too.

Well, that plan backfired in spectacular fashion. I lifted photos, letters, the entire contents of my old bedroom; he didn't notice anything missing. It's nothing to do with the fact he's blind. Dad's always been that blinkered. He only sees what he wants to see. The RUC was made for men like Frankie McCormack; men who always think they're in the right.

Dad'll tell you he was a great family man. I've heard him gurning about us to that Lithuanian fella. He's talked himself into believing his own crap. He wasn't bad to me or anything, but he was only nice when it suited him. When his mates were round, I was *Daddy's best girl, his wee angel.* Frankie always loved an audience. He was the same with Mummy, spinning everything to his own advantage. Sure, look at the song and dance he made of getting her a caravan. Mummy never asked for one. She preferred the Continent, some place you'd be guaranteed a bit of sun. It was Dad who had to be here in Ballycastle, for the fishing and that pub all his old cronies drank in. Dad always got his own way. He could usually convince Mum it was what she wanted too.

I was different. I saw right through him. I'm not even sure I loved my dad. He wasn't an easy man to love. I've mellowed now. It's hard to stay raging for thirty-five years. I wouldn't say I love him. It's more pity I feel. He's such a pathetic specimen. Look at him moping around that filthy caravan. Clinging to the past, when the past was far from perfect. I tried to help. I don't know what else I could've done. Don't believe what you see in films. It's harder than it looks to communicate from beyond the grave. Turns out, when it comes to haunting, I'm the silent, invisible type. I didn't see that coming. Before the bomb, I was the loudest girl in my class. Death's been a maturing experience for me, though I've developed a right knack for nicking shit.

It was boredom, or maybe frustration, which got me lifting other people's stuff. I suppose I felt sorry for them. They were all just as stuck as Dad. Now, don't be thinking I'm an angel or anything, helping everybody out. The idea of stirring also appealed; I've always liked messing with people's heads. I'm still a teenage girl at heart. I started with the deeds to Seacliff. I could see myself in Pete. He's young; the world's his oyster. He shouldn't be tying himself to this place. If I'd any choice in the matter, I certainly wouldn't be hanging around this hole. Then, I took the young ones' gadgets. They were coming between the kids and their mum. I felt for her. I miss my mummy something shocking. I wish I'd talked to her more. Things escalated quickly after that. It turns out people hoard the stupidest stuff. Nobody seems able to let anything go.

I mean, look at them all clambering about in the mud. Clinging on to a stupid tin box. It's undignified. It's not the empty caravan they're bothered about. It's all the stuff I've piled inside. Kathleen's photo. The fat one's drink. That wee skitter of a dog. Listen to the howls of it; it's like the Hound of the bloody Baskervilles. They can see their stuff through the window. They just can't get to it. They're heart-feared of it going over the cliff with the caravan. I wish they could see there's nothing worth keeping in there. I only nicked things that were holding them back.

Martha's different. People are always worth holding on to. I feel like screaming, *forget the bloody caravan. Youse need to find Martha.* She was such a sweetheart. When I was younger, I was in and out of her caravan all the time. I used to babysit her wee girls. Martha was always trying to feed me – buns, cakes, sausage rolls – her cupboards were coming down with treats. My mummy wasn't a baker. It was only packet biscuits in our house. I used to love Martha's caravan. It felt warm in there, like Christmas or something. Our caravan was always cold.

I should've been keeping a closer eye on Martha. Maybe I could've stopped this from happening. I'd noticed her wandering about as if she couldn't remember which caravan was hers. My gran went like that when she started doting. Once she spent an hour in the car park at Crazy Prices trying to get into somebody else's motor. She was in a right state by the time we found her. Martha's clearly gone the same way. Two days ago, I found her up here on the bench, staring at the sea like she was watching something out there. I knew it wasn't safe. There was bound to be an accident eventually. It's the world's dumbest place to put a bench. Typical Frankie McCormack, always insisting he knows best. Fingers crossed the wind blows it off the cliff tonight.

I take that back. If the bench goes it'll take Martha with it. She's just over the cliff edge, clinging on to a ledge. Any sudden movement would knock her off. She's petrified, poor thing, and foundered too. She's got nothing but a nightie on. It looks like the rest of them have forgotten her. They're preoccupied with the caravan. Selfish bastards. What are they thinking? It's only her husband who's still searching. It'd break your heart to hear him, shuffling about in his slippers, calling her name. John was always such a nice man. Quiet, but really kind. He only ever had eyes for his girls. I wish my dad had been more like him. I don't think Frankie even knew who I was.

I was fifteen the year I died. 1984: a long, muggy blur of a summer. It felt like September would never come. I was running about with two girls from the Fountain: Kelly-Anne and Denise. They were nice girls, though Dad didn't like me going over the Fountain. He said it wasn't safe. We were into boys and cider and Cyndi Lauper. All of us done our hair like hers. Back-combed, crimped, sprayed solid with Silvikrin; we must've looked like trolls. We didn't give a toss what people thought. We were girls and we just wanted to have fun. Given the state of Derry in the eighties, this was easier said than done. Any fun we had, we made ourselves: watching videos in Denise's bedroom, taking turns on her brother's Spectrum, reading the sexy bits in *Just Seventeen*.

I knew the Troubles were going on and that my dad was a legitimate target; everybody in the RUC was. I knew I was a Prod because I went to a Protestant school and that the IRA was for Catholics. I couldn't have told you much more than that. I was just like every other teenager. I'd no interest in politics. I was into music, make-up and myself. I'll tell you what I wasn't into. Caravan parks and scenery. I didn't appreciate Dad dragging me down to Seacliff. I wanted to stay with my mates in Derry. Now I'm spending eternity here.

I don't blame Dad for the car bomb. I can forgive him for forgetting to check the car. It wasn't him who put it there. It'd be easier to be angry about the bomb. But it's everything before that really hurts. All those years Dad didn't listen, when he only saw what he wanted to see. The way he made me in his image. *Daddy's wee princess.* Not the Lynette I really was. He's still at it. With the bench. And the caravan. And convincing that fella to pin it down. Don't believe him when he says it's all for me and Mummy. Frankie's first thought will always be himself.

The rain's coming down in sheets now. The caravan's begun to slide. They're all starting to panic. Even Trevor's swearing a bit. I'm watching Alma. I really like her. She has a bit of gumption about her. She's the kind of girl I was trying to be. Smart. Confident. Precocious. If only she was a bit more like her mum – head full of supernatural shite – she might've cracked the case. She was getting close. Eventually she'd have put two and two together and realized something wasn't adding up. I'd have let her get to me in the end.

It's too late now. The caravan's hanging over the edge. Nobody cares who took their stuff. They're just desperate to get it back. It'd be funny if it wasn't so sad. Kathleen's crying. Pete's battering the window with a tennis racquet. That looper in the tracksuit's trying to lift the caravan with his mind. His whole face has gone beetroot with the effort. He's going to give himself a stroke. What a bunch of losers. Why am I even helping them? They're incapable of seeing what's actually happening. This could be the fresh start they've been waiting for. Tomorrow everything could be different. They'd finally be able to move on.

While everybody's peching and grunting with the effort of holding the static down, Alma's still investigating.

She edges her way carefully from window to window, peering into the darkness with a torch. Once she's made a complete circuit of the caravan, she approaches Pete.

'Martha's not in there,' she announces. 'We need to go and find her.'

Pete isn't listening. He's busy shouting instructions to the others. He needs sandbags and a tow rope.

Alma repeats herself, louder this time, so everybody hears.

God, it's painful watching them. They're not bad people. They must know what they need to do. There's a little old lady out there, alone and scared, in the storm. She has to be the priority. But it's obvious, they're all struggling to think of Martha. The fear has made them mean. *Of course they're going to help with the search, they're coming the second they get their stuff back. A couple of minutes will hardly make any difference. There's no point panicking.* At least, that's what they're trying to tell themselves, but none of them are really buying it. Every face I look at's all screwed up with guilt. And fear. And desperation.

This lot need to let go *now*. But they can't. Or won't. Or don't know how to. They've been holding on for far too long.

Anna's trying to convince one of the foreign fellas he could get in via the skylight, when I hear John shout, 'Over here. I've found her.'

The old boy's already on his hands and knees, peering over the cliff edge, shining his torch into Martha's petrified face. 'Hold on, pet,' he says. 'Help's coming.' Help isn't coming. There's nothing behind him, nothing but darkness and driving rain. The poor man's exhausted from shock and cold. He tries to shout but can't manage anything more than a feeble yelp. Nobody hears him call. Nobody except me.

I know what I have to do. I can't be silent or invisible any longer. Martha needs me to make a scene. I use every ounce of energy I can muster. Now's the time to haunt like a proper ghost. I let the anger build up in my arms and legs until I slowly begin to rise, through the rain and wind, till I'm hovering above the cliff. When I'm fifteen, maybe twenty feet up, I bring my rage down in a furious rush. Thirty-five years of pent-up fury descends upon the stupid bench. I feel the wood splinter beneath me. I hear the crack as it splits in two. I come down so hard I might've left a crater. Tomorrow, they'll wonder what on earth's happened here, but I know exactly what I've done. I've severed the tie. I've brought an end to things. I've drawn a line my dad couldn't draw. I might not love him, but I can't watch him suffer. I have let him go.

I open my mouth and howl. The sound that comes out of me isn't human. It's sad and angry and urgent. I'm screaming for Martha. I'm screaming at Dad. I'm screaming for everything that's wrong with this place. I am screaming for the person I was going to be. I make myself impossible to ignore. Like a banshee screeching across the clifftop. My voice pierces the wind. It goes skimming across the damp grass until it reaches the people gathered around the caravan. For a second, they freeze, then turn as one to peer into the darkness.

'Did you hear that?' asks Pete.

'What was it?' asks Anna.

'It's Martha,' says Alma. 'We have to help her.'

Each of them glances back at the caravan. They take a last long look at its corrugated-metal walls, its PVC doors and foggy windows. They're considering everything it contains. What it will cost to walk away. They are wondering who they'll be tomorrow. If some vital part of themselves will be lost. Barely three seconds pass; five at most. Then, each one lifts their hands. Solemnly. Reverently. Silently. They step away from the caravan. They are choosing to let go.

Acknowledgements

A huge and heartfelt thank-you to Fiona Murphy and the team at Doubleday for indulging my love of caravans, and to my wonderful agents, Kate Johnson and Rachel Crawford, for their friendship, support and endless enthusiasm throughout the wilderness that was 2020.

Thanks to my Lockdown pal and fearless first reader, Michael Gould, and to Roisin O'Donnell and Cynan Jones for early advice and encouragement. Thanks and admiration also go out to all the artists who helped me re-create Seacliff on my dining-room wall when I couldn't make it up to the coast: Georgina and Natasha Garland, Milo Durnin, William Routh, Bee, Elsa and Will Rowlatt, Caoileann O'Rourke, Ynes Hawthorne, Elsie and Harry Parkes, and Anne Thwaites.

Finally, the biggest, loudest thank-you to the amazing team of actors who brought Seacliff and my stories to life on the radio – Patrick Buchanan, Roísín Gallagher, Chris Grant, Jo Donnelly, Ignacy Rybarczyk, Beccy Henderson, Seamus O'Hara, Carol Moore, Ian McElhinney and Dearbháile McKinney – and to Michael Shannon, who directed proceedings with incredible care and creativity.

This one's for anyone who's ever spent a wet weekend up the north coast in a caravan.

Jan Carson is a writer and community arts facilitator based in Belfast. Her first novel, *Malcolm Orange Disappears,* was published in 2014 to critical acclaim, followed by a short-story collection, *Children's Children* (2016), and two flash fiction anthologies, *Postcard Stories* (2017) and *Postcard Stories 2* (2020). Her second novel, *The Fire Starters* (2019), won the EU Prize for Literature and was shortlisted for the Dalkey Novel of the Year Award. Her work has appeared in numerous journals and on BBC Radio 3 and 4. She has won the *Harper's Bazaar* short-story competition and has been shortlisted for the BBC National Short Story Award and the Seán Ó Faoláin Short Story Prize. She specializes in running arts projects and events with older people, especially those living with dementia.